Understanding Shakespeare's plays in performance

JAY L. HALIO

Manchester
University Press

Distributed exclusively in the USA and Canada
by St. Martin's Press, New York

© JAY L. HALIO 1988

Published by
Manchester University Press
Oxford Road, Manchester, M13 9PL

*Distributed exclusively in the USA and Canada
by* St. Martin's Press, Room 400, 175 Fifth Avenue,
New York, NY 10010, USA

British Library cataloguing in publication data
Halio, Jay L.
    Understanding Shakespeare's plays in performance.
    1. Shakespeare, William—Dramatic production
    I. Title
    792.9'5   PR3091

Library of Congress cataloging in publication data applied for

ISBN 0-7190-2699-7 *hardback*

Typeset by
Koinonia Limited, Manchester
Printed in Great Britain by
Hartnolls Ltd, Bodmin, Cornwall

FOR
THOMAS CLAYTON

CONTENTS

ACKNOWLEDGEMENTS

Many people have helped, knowingly or otherwise, in the making of this book, which has grown out of a long experience in seeing Shakespeare's plays performed. Hence, my first debt is to the hundreds of actors, directors, set and costume designers, stage managers, box office officials, and others who collaborate in putting Shakespeare's plays on the boards. More immediately, the book has developed out of planning and leading a series of summer seminars for secondary school teachers on the topic, 'Shakespeare: Enacting the Text', funded by the National Endowment of the Humanities. To the fifteen teachers each year since the summer of 1985 who have joined me in Delaware and later at the Shakespeare Institute in Stratford-upon-Avon, I owe much for stimulating my thinking on how to approach Shakespeare's plays in performance.

Several friends and colleagues have read the manuscript as it evolved from first drafts to final version. My thanks for many useful suggestions and encouragement go to Marvin Rosenberg, Ronald Mulryne, James Bulman, Stanley Wells and Carol Carlisle. My greatest debt is to Thomas Clayton, who has graciously allowed me to dedicate the book to him. Whatever virtues this work may have, I owe largely to him and to the others who have taken both time and care to work through what I have written; the faults are all of my own making.

The chapter on 'Finding the Text' originally appeared in much different form in *Shakespeare Quarterly*, 35 (1985). Two other chapters, 'Finding the Set Design' and 'Finding the Subtext' appear as 'Images of Shakespeare: Contemporary Set Designs of Shakespeare's Plays' and 'Subtext in Shakespeare' in *Images of Shakespeare* (University of Delaware Press) and *Susquehanna University Studies* (Susquehanna University Press). I am grateful to the editors and publishers of these volumes for permission to use these materials here in a revised form. Quotations are keyed to the Riverside Shakespeare, edited by G. B. Evans.

Why this book?

Every year, hundreds of thousands of people buy tickets to see Shakespeare's plays performed – at Stratford-upon-Avon (England), Stratford-upon-Avon (Ontario), the National Theatre in London, the Oregon Shakespeare Festival, the San Diego Old Globe, the Old Globe of the Southwest, at nationally subsidized theatres in Munich, Budapest, Berlin, Paris, and virtually every corner of the world. No other playwright commands the kind of interest that Shakespeare does. After nearly four hundred years, one might expect audiences to grow weary of seeing the same plays over again. Just the opposite is true: the interest in them, far from declining, steadily increases. Why? What is so special about Shakespeare's plays that they are unrivalled in popularity by any others the world has known?

There are many answers to this question, most of them familiar but still compelling. Shakespeare tells us more about ourselves as human beings than any other dramatist or poet. Shakespeare's plays lend themselves to many interpretations, so that no single production can ever exhaust all the possibilities. Shakespeare's dramatic verse is the most sublime and moving, even in trans lation, that any dramatist has ever written. Shakespeare's charac ters are marvellously diverse and entertaining. And so forth.

Among the worst reasons for attending performances of the plays is the snob appeal that going to Shakespeare has for some theatregoers. Shakespeare is for everyone – the intellectual and the plebeian, the professional critic and the person who likes a good night out, the young and the old, the schoolchild trying to understand the text he has been assigned, and adults who pay their money to see an enjoyable show. Shakespeare's plays have something for everyone. In performance, moreover, they are much more accessible than they are when read from heavily annotated texts, for performances somehow provide all the annotation we need, or enough of it; they make the plays live.

After a good performance of one of the plays – *Hamlet*, perhaps, or *As You Like It* – most theatregoers will say they enjoyed the experience. They may not be able to say quite why they did, but they know what they liked, or at least they know that they liked it. This book is designed not merely to help theatregoers know what it is they liked (or disliked), but *why* they did. By helping theatregoers understand the challenges involved in producing plays, it also sets out to afford a greater appreciation of the results. It is written, in other words, out of the conviction that the more we know and understand about what happens and why, the fuller the experience will be, and the greater the impact the performance will have.

The impact will be greater partly because the more an audience understands, the more responsive it is likely to be, and the more responsive an audience is, the more fully realized the production is apt to become. No acting company likes a cold house. A responsive audience, by contrast, acts upon the performers in such a way as to evoke the best that is in them. Lively and inspiring theatre may not require well-informed and responsive audiences, but it is certainly aided and abetted by them.

Recognizing that no performance of any Shakespeare play can be definitive, owing to the rich complexity and ambiguity the text contains, this book provides no recipes for productions or formulae for critical judgements. It supplies, rather, a number of questions that should help audiences inquire more deeply into the nature of their experiences during and after witnessing a Shakespeare play in performance. While every production will be more or less different from every other one of the same play, the essential questions do not vary much. Struck by major adaptations of the text, the thoughtful spectator will inquire into other alterations to understand the implications the changes have for interpretation, for the rationale of the production. He or she will question the set design, the transposition of the time frame from one period to another (if that happens), and the effect the transposition has on the production. Character interpretation will vary, sometimes greatly, from one production to another, and the inquiring theatregoer will question the differences and the ways these interpretations can – or cannot – be justified. Having heard about the 'subtexts' actors use to interpret their roles, theatregoers naturally will want to know more about what they are and how they function. If subtexts are the meanings lying beneath or between the lines that indicate to actors the way to speak them, how are they found? The way verse and prose are rendered in performance is also important; is there anything special we need to know about understanding their difficulties or intricacies? Spectacle, stage business, musical and other effects have a prominent place in many productions today: what do they contribute to, or how do they detract from, the plays?

Finally, is the overall interpretation of a play in performance successful, and if so, in what terms? In this age of ideology, it may be essential to ask if ideology has a necessary place in Shakespearean production, or if it tends to reduce the plays to propaganda. We enjoy Shakespeare: will we enjoy his plays more, or less, if there is a particular slant given to them by the director or designer? What means are available to help us analyze performances so that we can properly understand and then judge the significance of the production? How can we know whether we are seeing Shakespeare performed or something that passes under the name of Shakespeare but is really something else, not Shakespeare at all? These are a few of the general questions this book addresses. In each chapter, more specific questions are raised, most of them having to do with specific productions that are described and discussed. Again, there is no attempt to be definitive. The questions are essentially suggestive. The alert reader and theatregoer will think of many others, some related to those mentioned here and others not.

To emphasize the questioning, not answering, nature of this book, every chapter title begins with 'Finding'. One finds what one looks for, of course, but without some knowledge of what kinds of thing to look for, one is likely to miss a great deal. Hence, the reader will notice chapters on 'Finding the Text', 'Finding the Set Design', 'Finding the Characters', 'Finding the Subtext', 'Finding the Language', 'Finding the Stage Business, Music, and Other Effects', and 'Finding Coherence: The Overall Interpretation'. 'Finding' is used in a special sense here. It means 'making discoveries

about', and it involves a process that sharpens a playgoer's awareness of some important aspects of a performance. Take, for example, the matter of 'finding' the text of a particular production (see
Chapter I). The first step is realizing that the script used in the
theatre is never precisely the same as the text published in whatever edition the playgoer may have read. There will always be a
certain amount of change made by a theatrical editor, adaptor, or
script 'doctor': words, lines, perhaps whole speeches and, in some
cases, whole scenes will be deleted; sometimes a modern word
will be substituted for a word that the editor considers archaic or
otherwise undesirable; occasionally there will be transpositions
of speeches or scenes to create a new pattern of structure or meaning; in extreme cases there will be additions to the original text,
whether in the form of songs, extended pantomimes, or actual
dialogue. Playgoers who realize the kinds of things that can go on
during the preparation of a script for the theatre are less likely, in
seeing a production, to accept without question any altered
interpretation that may result from the editing or adapting. On
the other hand, the more keenly aware playgoers are of the changes
that have been made in the text, the more they may appreciate
alterations that have sharpened some important point in the play
without destroying other important points. A well-informed
theatregoer will realize, too, that even the best available scholarly
texts may not reflect what Shakespeare intended to be staged at
any given time.

Thus to 'find' the text of a particular production is to find out
and take note of the relationship between the script that has been
used in the production and the text of the play as it is generally
read. Consider another example: to 'find' the set design (discussed
in Chapter II), playgoers must know something about the variety
of visual treatments that have been considered appropriate for
Shakespeare's plays over the years. They can then begin to understand the challenges faced by the director and designer in deciding
upon the period, place, and style for their sets and costumes.
Playgoers should realize that there may be valid reasons for the
startling and seemingly arbitrary choices made in some modern
productions, but they should be aware, too, of the potential dangers
as well as advantages that innovative designs offer. To 'find' the
set design of a particular production is to reflect upon the possible
reasons for the design that has been used and to decide whether
or not the experience of the play is thereby enriched or distorted

by the visual elements of the production. In a similar way, theatre-goers may 'find' the characters and other aspects of a production that are discussed in other chapters of this book. The process always involves an increased awareness of what has taken place – and why – in the preparation of the production, then the discovery of previously unnoticed significances, and, finally, an informed judgement about the value of what has been done.

The chapters of this book are linked progressively but are not so tightly connected that one cannot dip into any single chapter without having read what precedes it. The first chapter, on finding the text, assumes that the text, or script, of the play is primary, the place where any production – and therefore any performance – begins. On the other hand, some productions may be so heavily influenced by an image or design (to which the text is later adapted) that production may be said to begin there instead. Character and subtext are intimately connected, but I have separated these topics into two chapters in order to treat character generally and subtext more specifically. Stage business, music, lighting, and other effects are probably the least essential aspects of Shakespearean production, notwithstanding the fact that Shakespeare's own stage directions often indicate gestures or other 'business'; that gestures are often indispensable adjuncts to character interpretation; and that music was an important component of many scenes as Shakespeare wrote them.

After these different aspects of production have been considered, questions naturally arise: What do we have? What does everything add up to? How does everything fit into an overall interpretation that gives, or fails to give, a production its unity and coherence? Or are unity and coherence as essential as we think? Can they be worth sacrificing for something else?

Another way of regarding what this book sets out to do is to think of attending a rehearsal of a play. During rehearsals, various aspects of staging and interpretation are worked out. The director and the actors together try to figure out the best means of presenting a scene or part of a scene. The actors will try one way, then another, then still another way of acting until they discover what works best, given the subtext, language problems, exigencies of staging, overall interpretation, and other considerations. In the process, one becomes aware of the many aspects of presenting Shakespeare that in performance might never become evident. Nor should they. But being on the inside, as it were, provides a new perspective, an insight into the complexities of production that cannot help but inform our judgement even as it illuminates our understanding. Afterwards, we come to a regular performance not only with greater expectation and anticipation, but with a better grasp of what the production is all about and how it got that way.

If this book succeeds in its goals, then, its readers will arrive at performances of Shakespeare's plays with the kind of awareness that someone who has attended any of the rehearsals might have gained. Perforce the approach the book most often takes is to recognize and understand the problems of production from the inside out, that is, from the director's, actor's, designer's conception of what is at stake. For a better understanding of the processes of producing the plays should lead to a better grasp of the production in all of its aspects and ultimately to a greater enjoyment of the experience. The more we know, the more we understand, the more our appreciation of performance will be enhanced.

This book will not make performances better. It is not written for the producer, director, designer, or actor. If it takes their part at times, it is only to allow the reader some access to what is happening as a production takes shape and then finds its place on the boards. Nor is this book in any sense 'required reading' for the enjoyment of Shakespeare. Audiences have gone to countless performances in the past, as they will in the future, without any such guidance and have found the experiences worthwhile. Shakespeare in performance is accessible without guidebooks, just as the wonders of Florence or Athens can be enjoyed without a Baedecker. But with a Baedecker, the experience is deepened, enhanced, illuminated. Let this book, then, become a modest guide to traveling in the wonderfully varied territories that are Shakespeare's plays.

CHAPTER I

Finding the text

Imagine going to a performance of *Hamlet*, sitting back in your seat, and waiting for the play to start. Instead of the scene on the ramparts with Horatio and the guards peering into the cold, unfriendly night, the production begins with Claudius addressing the court. What happened to scene one? Where are the first Ghost scene and Horatio's ineffectual attempt to deal with the spectre that has been haunting the ramparts for several nights past? Why are we thrust immediately into scene two of the play?

Good questions, and they were among those aroused by the Oxford-Cambridge Players' production of *Hamlet*, directed by Jonathan Miller about fifteen years ago. Most of the information contained in the first scene is inessential to the plot, as Miller doubtless recognized when he cut it. But streamlining the text, or acting script, may have been only one of several considerations he had in mind — and that not the most important one — in making his choice. When the Ghost finally appeared at the end of Act I, he was a very friendly Ghost, sitting on a bench or log disconsolately telling young Hamlet his story — a story designed to elicit the utmost sympathy from the young man. If the first scene had been retained, an entirely different conception of the Ghost would have been necessary — something closer to the ghastly spook we usually see.

Deleting the first scene of *Hamlet*, moreover, altered the entire structure of Act I. It greatly reduced the effect produced by the Ghost and Hamlet groping towards each other from the chasm that separates the living and the dead.[1] In other words, by cutting the text here and elsewhere, Miller had changed the play; some would say he had changed its essential nature. Was the play any longer Shakespeare's? Had Miller adapted it so radically by cutting the text that he had, in effect, offered his audience a different play?

These are important questions, not only for critics and theatre historians, but for thoughtful, intelligent theatregoers goers, too. What is it that we see when we attend a Shakespearean play? Do we get authentic Shakespeare, or someone else's very different version of what Shakespeare originally wrote? How can we come to grips with the issue? What kinds of evidence can we bring to bear to help us determine whether a production of *Hamlet* or *King Lear* or *As You Like It* is a legitimate Shakespearean production – or something else?

Before attempting to answer those questions, we may need some background information about the nature of Shakespeare's texts. The problem may at first seem highly complicated, but once we understand it we will be in a much better position to grapple with the issues of legitimacy and authenticity. We need to realize at the outset that what Shakespeare wrote is not always easy to establish. And what he wrote he may have later revised, either for a specific occasion or for some other reason. Although some scholars have long believed that a single text once existed for every Shakespeare play, this notion has recently been heavily discredited. The text of *King Lear*, for example, is now accepted by many as existing in two significantly different Shakespearean forms: an early quarto printed in 1608 that may derive from Shakespeare's manuscript, and a later revised version published in the great folio of 1623, the first collected edition of Shakespeare's plays.[2] The distinctions between the two versions – the inconsistencies in characterizations, for example, or certain structural problems – are obscured in most modern editions, which conflate, or splice, the texts, combining what is unique in each one into a play Shakespeare never saw performed.

The text of *Hamlet* is even more complicated. It exists in three different forms: the first quarto (Q1), published in 1603; a second quarto (Q2), published the following year; and the folio text (F). Q1 appears to be the least authoritative version of the three, and many scholars suspect that it is a pirated, or unauthorized, text – a shortened version of Shakespeare's play that was taken on tour; but its provenance is still debated.[3] Q2 derives from Shakespeare's manuscript and therefore has the greatest authority; it also is the longest version of the play. F is shorter than Q2 and may derive from a transcript of Shakespeare's manuscript that contained his revisions or, as some scholars have argued, from a playhouse manuscript or promptbook.[4] F not only makes cuts but adds some lines and alternative readings, such as 'solid' for Q1, Q2 'sallied' (usually emended to 'sullied') in Hamlet's first soliloquy ('that this too, too solid flesh,' etc., I.ii). Since both Q2 and F are authoritative, or substantive, texts, modern editors typically conflate the two, occasionally taking over some readings from Q1, thus making a completely eclectic text. Again, what results in most modern editions is an overlong *Hamlet* that Shakespeare never saw or expected to see!

Even those plays that have come down to us in only one form, such as *Macbeth*, which was printed only in the folio, may once have existed in an earlier, different state, now lost, as J. M. Nosworthy has maintained.[5] Either Shakespeare or someone else may have revised or adapted the plays for performance some time after their original presentation. Now, this is a common theatrical practice, one that continues to the present time. Even a new play performed rarely resembles the manuscript the author first drafted, and revivals of old plays often are altered to fit different times or places. We need not accept the comment of Shakespeare's first editors, Heminges and Condell, who compiled the folio of 1623, that their late colleague scarcely blotted a line. Ben Jonson's endorsement of that view in his remark, 'Would he had blotted a thousand', should also be regarded with scepticism. However swift his composition was, Shakespeare was subject, like other mortals, to second thoughts and to the exigencies involved in actually mounting plays for performance.

If, therefore, the evidence from multiple-text plays shows that neither Shakespeare nor his fellows regarded his scripts as beyond revision or in any sense untouchable, what limits should be observed by producers or directors who must provide a lively, authentic, but above all relevant and entertaining performance for a modern audience? Or are these qualifications mutually exclusive? And where does the playgoer stand in all this? What criteria should he or she use to judge the production of a Shakespearean text?

'Cut, abbreviate, and slice again, as much as you want. The more you discard from the text, the better,' wrote Boris Pasternak to Grigori Kozintsev in October 1953, when the Russian director was preparing a stage production of *Hamlet*. 'I always regard half the text of any play, of even the most immortal and classic work of genius as a diffused remark that the author wrote in order to acquaint actors as thoroughly as possible with the heart of the action to be played. As soon as a theatre has penetrated his artistic intention, and mastered it, one can and should sacrifice the most vivid and profound lines (not to mention the pale and indifferent ones), provided that the actors have achieved an equally talented performance of an acted, mimed, silent, or laconic equivalent to these lines of the drama and in this part of its development.'[6]

Few theatre directors would go as far as Pasternak recommended, and certainly Kozintsev, who was using Pasternak's translation, did not. Thanking the writer for his permission to 'cut and slice', he astutely observed that while he might completely agree with the advantages of 'acted, mimed, silent, or laconic equivalents', these really required a screen. 'In the cinema,' he responded, 'with its power of visual imagery, it would be possible to risk achieving equal forcefulness. On the stage, the spoken word is king. . . .'[7]

King or not, the text of Shakespeare's plays has often been dethroned, not only in the interest of speeding up performance time (and allowing for intermissions – unknown in Shakespeare's Globe Theatre), but also in the interest of providing new or original interpretations – the sort of thing that the eminent theatre historian and critic, Muriel St. Clare Byrne, wrote against in a powerful essay called 'Dramatic Intention and Theatrical Realization'.[8] The issue clearly centres on the terms of her title: when the theatrical realization does not match the intention of the play, we have a distortion or, in politer terms, an adaptation of the text. But this response may beg the question, since the dramatic intention itself is subject to interpretation. Shakespeare's plays being complex works of art, they are open to various and sometimes conflicting interpretations. Cutting or otherwise altering the text – transposing passages or scenes, adding characters or even dialogue – may help simplify the text and clarify the interpretation; but taken too far, these strategies may become counterproductive. The question again arises, how far is too far?

In a recent essay, Thomas Clayton has explored the implications of the question in great detail, using a number of productions, Shakespearean and otherwise, as illustrations. He concludes:

> If there is a finite range of 'legitimate productions' of Shakespeare's plays, it is not easily defined, because theatrical performance involves at least two orders of analysis and evaluation that do not necessarily and in practice very often do not coincide: they center on the meaning(s) of the script and on the significance of performance. . . . In fact, the dialectic of meaning and significance must come into play at a premiere production, since there is invariably some tension between script and performance that has finally to be resolved in favor of the latter; the greater distance of the playwright from his or her performers and audience, both metaphorically and in actual production, the greater the tension is likely to be.[9]

The dialectic between meaning and significance is precisely the issue. What a play meant for its author and its original audience may be quite different from what it signifies in contemporary production, as Clayton notes, and it may be impossible (it usually is) to recover all of those original meanings. The question then becomes how far from the original sense the modern production drifts or is driven. Or, to put the question in other terms: without going to the extreme that Pasternak advocated, how free can producers or directors feel to adapt the text of Shakespeare's plays and still remain within boundaries that preserve the plays' essential structure and meaning?

Merely transposing the time and setting of a Shakespeare play, as in Joseph Papp's production of *Much Ado About Nothing* (directed by A. J. Antoon), which was set at the turn of this century in a middle American town, does not in itself seriously alter any essential aspect of the play, even as it provides the play with a fresh look. However, alterations such as these are sometimes accompanied by others much more radical that do change the nature of the play. I am not talking here about clear-cut adaptations of the plays in the form of musical comedies, like *Kiss Me Kate!* or the late seventeenth-century transformation of *A Midsummer Night's Dream* into an opera called *The Fairy Queen*. The distant relation of these works to Shakespeare's originals is indicated by their different titles. In these instances, there is no real attempt to follow Shakespeare; his plays become, rather, springboards for the development of other artefacts. Much of the same thing can be said of certain film renditions of the plays, as Kozinstev has suggested and as his own superbly imaginative films of *Hamlet* and *King Lear* attest. Different media require different approaches. But where the medium remains the theatre (or as in the case of television productions like the BBC series, a deliberate approximation to it), then analysis and evaluation begin by recognizing not only the external trappings of the production (set design, costume, etc.), the actors' performances, and the overall interpretation of the play, but also the alterations to the text. It is these alterations that can and inevitably do affect the play's dramatic structure, the actors' performances (even the appearance or omission of some roles), and the overall interpretation that the director has adopted and the production exhibits. As Trevor Nunn has said of directing *Hamlet*, 'When you approach the text of *Hamlet*, the cutting is virtually the production. What you decide to leave in is your version of the play.'[10]

Let us consider a case in more detail. A highly controversial play as many now regard it, *The Merchant of Venice* is rarely performed without significant cuts and other alterations of the text that help to meliorate if not eliminate the anti-Semitism that it contains. A key passage is Shylock's long aside that expresses his feelings about Antonio (I.iii.41-52). It includes the line, 'I hate him for he is a Christian.' Omission of the passage is usually a clear indication of how the director has conceived Shylock's role – and with it, much else in the play. The script is then tailored accordingly, so that Shylock can emerge, as in Henry Irving's famous portrayal, as a tragic hero.[11] This was not John Barton's conception in the two Royal Shakespeare Company productions he directed, either the first at The Other Place, with Patrick Stewart as Shylock (1978), or the second in the main house with David Suchet in the role (1981). The actors presented significantly different portrayals of Shylock, but they were far closer to each other than they were to, say, Laurence Olivier's portrayal in Jonathan Miller's National Theatre production mentioned earlier. Both saw Shylock as a bad human being and a bad Jew (Stewart perhaps more so than Suchet) and did not try to gloss over his faults; the long aside in I.iii was accordingly retained. At one point, Stewart struck Jessica very hard across the face, thus providing further motivation for her elopement. At the end, Stewart's acceptance of his life and half his fortune was much more obsequious than Suchet's more reluctant but still considered acquiescence.[12]

Miller's production revived much of the nineteenth century's approach; his production was, in fact, set in the nineteenth century. Shylock, in striped trousers and frock coat, appeared as an alien figure trying very hard to gain acceptance into the upper crust of Victorian society. This was the time, after all, of Baron Rothschild's exclusion from the House of Commons, to which he had been duly elected.[13] No place here for Shylock's aside in I.iii, or for that matter the low comedy of Launcelot Gobbo and much else in the play. On the other hand, the casket scenes in Belmont involving Morocco and Arragon, often cut in eighteenth-century productions, were retained and made as comical as possible to point up the snobbishness that Portia and her stratum of society represented. Most of the dialogue involving Jessica was deleted, especially the scenes concerning her elopement. Unlike the situation portrayed in the BBC-TV film or John Barton's production at The Other Place, Jessica's marriage to Lorenzo in this production was hardly a joyous escape from a detested life ('Our house is hell'). The actual elopement amidst the merriment of masking in II.vi was entirely omitted. Instead, Jessica soon afterwards appeared troubled by her action, and at the end of the play she did not join the other happy couples but remained alone on stage after Antonio's exit or, in the televised version, drifted away from Portia's house, her father's deed in her hand, as an unseen cantor (in voice-over) intoned the mourner's 'Kaddish'.

Thus Miller shaped a quite different version of *The Merchant of Venice* from the one Shakespeare originally wrote. Excellent theatre, perhaps, but was it Shakespeare?[14] Joseph Papp similarly has been known to take liberties with Shakespeare's texts – his production of *The Two Gentlemen of Verona* evolved from Shakespeare's modest pastoral play into a rock opera with a multi-ethnic cast that won awards as well as box office appeal. Like many contemporary producers, Papp has a healthy disregard for pedantry that can lead him far from the original texts, but at other times his productions – for all of their divergences – may succeed in bringing us closer to the spirit of Shakespeare's plays. They can and often do reveal hitherto unsuspected or underemphasized motifs, characterizations, and interrelationships. The 1972 production of *Much Ado About Nothing* altered the time and place of the original, but in the process no violence was done to Shakespeare's basic creation, which thus became more accessible to American audiences. A completely new musical score was composed to be more consistent with the new time and setting and was in itself delightful. Some cutting of the text was apparent, but not excessive: director A. J. Antoon kept the *essentials* intact. Although the dialogue in many scenes was more or less curtailed, wholesale cutting of scenes or characters or major transpositions were not the rule here as they were in Miller's *Merchant*. Some new scenes were added, such as the barber-shop scene alluded to at III.ii.43-50, or rather new sets (tantamount to new scenes), such as the bathtub scene between Benedick and Claudio in the first act, where they discuss Claudio's attraction to Hero. These helped to enliven the action, but except for cries of 'Lemonade!' in the opening scene, there was no new dialogue. Beatrice, played by Kathleen Widdoes, appeared as a sprightly young woman of her time, her outspokenness underlined by her daring to sneak a cigarette and other bits of added stage business. But throughout she remained Shakespeare's Beatrice, and in her scene with Don Pedro (II.i.323-350) she showed a touching sensitivity and tactfulness that were matched only by her partner in the dialogue. I cannot recall another production that focused so well on their relationship to each other or that brought out so clearly what is in the text but can quite easily be lost.[15]

Given the fact that directors of Shakespeare's plays are apt to make alterations in the text – sometimes very drastic ones, such as those in Jonathan Miller's *Hamlet* and *Merchant of Venice* – how are theatregoers to know where and how the script of the performance differs from the received text, the one that typically appears in modern editions? Comparison between the acting script and the standard text is easy enough when the acting script is available, but usually it is not. At one time it was customary to publish acting editions, which made comparisons very simple. In the Restoration and for a century or more afterwards, acting editions of *Hamlet*, for example, often carried a note such as the following from the text printed in 1676 by Andrew Clark for J. Martyn and H. Herringman: 'This Play being too long to be conveniently Acted, such places as might be least prejudicial to the Plot or Sense, are left out upon the Stage: but that we may no way wrong the incomparable Author, are here inserted according to the Original Copy with this Mark".'[16] The tradition of publishing acting versions with significant alterations marked has since faded, replaced by the tradition of publishing annotated scholarly texts and school editions. These have generally ignored production exigencies and other aspects of staging, except when they contain a brief stage history, as in the Yale Shakespeare, although some of the newer editions, such as the New Cambridge and the New Oxford Shakespeare, are attempting to remedy this deficiency.[17]

Occasionally, as in Rosamund Gilder's record of John Gielgud's *Hamlet* (New York: Oxford University Press, 1937), we have a detailed account of the play as it was acted in a particular production. But even in this otherwise excellent and very useful volume a collation with the full text is missing, so that readers have to determine for themselves what has been deleted and then speculate upon the reasons. It is easy to understand, for instance, why Gielgud deleted all but seven lines of the scene with Reynaldo, but why were lines 45-53 of Act III, scene i, which include Claudius's significant aside, omitted? Was the cut made to suggest that Claudius was a more hardened villain than he appears up to now in Shakespeare's full text, the Q2 version? Gilder's running commentary on the action ignores the cut and, indeed, one has to remember the full text to notice that the lines are gone. Perhaps in an edition as full of apparatus as Gilder's, a full text with inverted commas indicating omissions would be too clumsy. Still, some indication of how Gielgud adapted his text would be useful.[18] By contrast, the text of *Hamlet* published for the BBC-TV series, *The Shakespeare Plays*, indicates quite clearly by means of a vertical rule and a marginal notation where the cuts are.[19]

Without such aids, to find the text of a production we may require a pretty complete knowledge of the play or at least be familiar with its essential passages, that is, those elements that are central to the dramatic structure or development of major themes and characters. Does this mean that serious, thoughtful theatregoers need to 'brush up their Shakespeare' before seeing a production, study the text in detail and even memorize key passages? While all that would help, a reasonable familiarity with the text may be all that is necessary. The missing first scene of *Hamlet*, the example with which we began, will strike most theatregoers at all familiar with the play. Similarly, the insertion of Shakespeare's Sonnet 116 ('Let me not to the marriage of true minds / Admit impediments') at the end of Romeo and Juliet's wedding scene (II.vi) in Michael Kahn's 1986 production will also strike theatregoers familiar with either the play or the sonnet as an interpolation to the text.[20]

Obviously, it would be asking too much of the non-specialist to acquire extensive knowledge of textual alterations of this sort; even professors of English sometimes have difficulty finding the text. On the other hand, where theatregoers suspect that a production has moved well beyond Shakespeare's original script, they may wish to consult a good edition afterwards and, trusting to memory as well as to competent reviews, see what happened. Analysis and evaluation, based upon such evidence as can be brought to bear from the production and comparison with the text, can prove very enlightening. They can help clarify for the theatregoer what the director's intentions were vis-à-vis those of Shakespeare's play. Nor need we immediately conclude that a 'distortion', that is, a radical alteration of the text, is all bad. By shifting the focus and removing some parts of the text, directors may help us to see more clearly some aspects of the play that otherwise may remain hidden or obscure. Or they may choose to highlight some aspects at the expense of others, as directors often do with the ending of *Romeo and Juliet*, which tends to soften the full impact of the young lovers' deaths. Not everything Shakespeare included in his manuscripts needs to be performed, as his own theatre company understood. The questions remain what they have always been: If this goes, then what are the consequences? Can they be justified, and if so, how?

Postscript on film productions

Filming Shakespeare's plays, as Kozintsev recognized, may permit – even require – heavy cutting of the text insofar as the director must translate Shakespeare's verbal images into visual ones. Franco Zeffirelli cut nearly sixty per cent of the text of *Romeo and Juliet* in making his film version without a corresponding shortening of the playing time. Among some of the famous passages he deleted are Juliet's soliloquy in III.i ('Gallop apace, you fiery-footed steeds') along with most of the rest of that scene and her later contemplation upon being entombed (IV.iii). For neither cut, however, did the camera substitute for the text as it does, for example, for the Friar's speech at the beginning of II.iii when he is picking herbs. Perhaps Zeffirelli was influenced by Olivia Hussey's inexperience as a Shakespearean actress or felt that Juliet's impassioned love for Romeo and, generally, her lively imagination were sufficiently conveyed without these speeches. In any event, some of Juliet's depth of character is sacrificed by these omissions. Of greater significance is the changed ending. John Russell Brown has written perceptively of the stage production (upon which the film was based); he noted how the heavy cuts in Shakespeare's text were replaced by 'dignified dumb shows of grief'. But, as Brown says, these could not compensate for the 'socially responsible particularity' of Shakespeare's lines.[21] Similarly, mainly through heavy deletions of text, the film's ending all but eliminated Shakespeare's emphasis upon reconciliation and accentuated instead the hatred and bitterness that had been uppermost in the director's interpretation from the start.[22]

Just as films tend to remove large amounts of Shakespeare's text, they also tend to make additions, not of lines so much as of stage business, scenic effects, and especially visual interpolations that tend to emphasize the director's interpretation of the text. This is not always a matter of translation from one medium to another and, as we have seen, stage productions sometimes make interpolations, too.[23] Laurence Olivier's film of *Richard III* begins, like Colley Cibber's stage version, before the action of Shakespeare's first act, borrowing a bit from the end of *Henry VI, Part 3*, and introduces the silent but quite conspicuous role of Jane Shore, King Edward's mistress, played by Pamela Brown.[24] In his film of *King Lear*, Peter Brook substituted for the opening dialogue between Gloucester and Kent a long, silent series of frames panning over the faces of expectant subjects, until the camera finally came to rest first on the back of Lear's throne, then on his grim countenance. Only then did the film's dialogue begin. In the storm scenes, moreover, to underscore his vision of the unfolding chaos, Brook introduced shots of hordes of drowned rats.

Kozintsev's film version of *Hamlet* opens with the Prince riding swiftly up to Elsinore Castle from Wittenberg, and Olivier's earlier film of the same play takes advantage of the available technology to provide inserts within frames. For example, as Ophelia tells her distressing story of Hamlet's visit to her chamber (II.i), we actually see what she describes in an insert. Again, as Horatio reads Hamlet's letter (IV.vi), we see through an insert Hamlet boarding the pirate ship and grappling with the pirates as the ships separate. In Kozintsev's film of *King Lear* Lear addresses not one but many Bedlam beggars in the third act, and in keeping with the social emphasis of the film, his speech on the 'poor naked wretches' is delivered in the context of those poor unfortunates who share with him his poor shelter. As a final touch, the Fool is still around at the end of the film, rudely kicked aside by the soldiers bearing off the bodies of Lear and Cordelia, after which he poignantly resumes playing his pipe.

Going still further afield from these productions, we may note the films by the great Japanese director, Akira Kurosawa. His adaptations of *Macbeth* and *King Lear*, *Throne of Blood* and *Ran*, respectively, are masterpieces of translation, not only from one medium to another, but from one culture to another. Kozinstev's films, by comparison, stick more closely to Shakespeare's texts, his additions and other alterations to the text notwithstanding; Kurosawa completely reconstitutes the plays. The Gloucester sub-plot, for example, cannot be found in *Ran*, and the three daughters are replaced by three sons. In *Throne of Blood*, fatalism rather than diabolism takes over, and the sterility of the Macbeths is made literal.[25]

The exigencies of television production centre primarily upon the smaller screen, which somewhat limits the scope of its visuals as opposed to the large screen of films. The contrast is nowhere more obvious than in the productions of *King Lear* for television by either Granada (with Laurence Olivier) or the BBC (with Michael Hordern) and the Cinemascope technology used by Grigori Kozintsev for his film. It is impossible, it seems, to convey the epic sweep of the play on television, and neither television production attempted to do what both Brook and Kozintsev achieved in different ways. Both mediums have a signal advantage over stage productions that they exploit sometimes to excess, it is true, but most often to excellent effect. This is, of course, the use of the closeup. Through this device, film and television can convey subtleties and intimacies much more difficult to attain on stage, particularly in large auditoriums, such as the main stage at Stratford-upon-Avon, England. And both mediums employ special effects not otherwise available to live stage performances, such as zoom focusing, overhead shots, unusual back lighting (for example, as used for Edgar's entrance as Edmund's opponent in V.iii in the BBC-TV version of *Lear*), and deliberate blurring or hallucinatory effects.

On the whole, however, both film and television tend to cling to realism as their dominant mode of representation. Hence, the producer of the BBC-TV *As You Like It* opted for an actual forest setting, and all of the forest scenes were shot in the vicinity of Glamis Castle, Scotland. But perhaps the most significant difference between watching a film or television production and watching a live stage performance is that on film we can see only what the director or editor intends us to see. On stage, we are freer to focus our attention where we please, to accept or reject the domination of an actor's delivery, except as the lighting designer may occasionally limit our freedom. Again, film and television productions are frozen in time; stage productions tend to evolve and change, sometimes drastically, during the run of performances, often growing in strength and sureness, but seldom so fixed that new insights and illuminations cannot be introduced and enjoyed.

CHAPTER II

Finding the set design

Anyone attending the Royal Shakespeare Company's performances of Shakespeare's plays in the last few years will recognize the justice of Ralph Berry's recent comment that designer's theatre has taken over from director's theatre.[1] The lavish settings, elaborate costuming, and intricate stage business rival all but the most extravagant Victorian representations associated with names like Henry Irving and Herbert Beerbohm Tree. Increasingly, as the 1985 season showed, designers – working closely with directors – have tended to set the plays in periods far removed from their original historical or chronological period. The design for *As You Like It* emphasized a stylized modern decor with nary a tree in Arden; *Troilus and Cressida* was set in the period of the Crimean War; and *The Merry Wives of Windsor*, as the programme format and notes made clear, was set precisely in 1959.

The Royal Shakespeare Company has not been alone, by any means, in the tendency to place Shakespearean plays in unexpected settings. In the same year, 1985, a deliberate violation of historical period was evident in several other theatres, including the National Theatre in London and the Shakespeare Theatre at the Folger in Washington, D. C. Nor is this tendency of recent origin, though it may have become particularly prevalent in recent years. In the past there have been many examples of either modern-dress productions or productions that have imposed strange new settings on familiar plays – for example, Orson Welles's 'voodoo' *Macbeth* (Lafayette Theatre, New York, 1936) and the American Civil War setting for *Troilus and Cressida* (American Shakespeare Festival, Stratford, Connecticut, 1957).

In Shakespeare's time, of course, things were different. Scenery was sparse – a bed thrust forward, a throne discovered, etc. Flying machines may have been used for Middleton's failed play, *The Witch*, and the consequent revival of *Macbeth* at the Blackfriars, but these were extraordinary pieces of stagecraft, intended to amuse a sophisticated, even decadent audience.[2] Much more attention was directed to costumes, which could be and often were rich and costly. Nor was much heed given to the particular historical period of the play. Then, as for many years afterwards, actors performed in the costume of their own period, whether the time of the play was the era of republican Rome (as in *Coriolanus* or *Julius Caesar*) or the reign of King Lear. This fact has sometimes been noted as a lack of historical sense on the part of Shakespeare and his fellows, but the truth may lie elsewhere, away from an inhibiting literal-mindedness (as other aspects of Elizabethan drama reveal) and closer to a sense of the contemporary significance of the action. Thus we find as late as the Restoration and eighteenth century actors still performing Shakespeare's plays in the dress of their own period, sporting large wigs, handsome swords and bucklers, and revealing hose as they walked along the Roman Forum or took their places in the court of Duke Theseus of Athens. Presumably, if Romans or Athenians could be made to speak in English blank verse, they could also be permitted to wear clothing of similar accent.

In the nineteenth century a change began in the direction of promoting as much historical accuracy as possible and culminating in the 'archaeological' productions of Charles Kean. There, not only the costumes and sets but all the props (weapons, utensils, etc.) were carefully researched and reproduced to match those of the supposed period in which the events took place, and programme notes gave scholarly justification in support of what was done. After all, Shakespearean productions were supposed to be an educational experience! The turning point is sometimes regarded as the production of *King John* staged by Charles Kemble in 1823, with Charles Young as the king and Kemble as the Bastard. John Robinson Planché designed the costumes and believed that by scrupulously adopting the style of the thirteenth century, in which the action is set, he completely reformed the prevailing tradition of costume design. By the end of the century, a reaction set in. William Poel and after him Harley Granville-Barker in the early twentieth century advocated a return to the simpler staging of the Elizabethan theatre and away from the impositions created by the proscenium stage and its heavy reliance upon 'pictorial' representation. While Poel tended to abandon scenery altogether, Granville-Barker formalized and stylized it and introduced imaginative costumes and lighting. Conservative critics complained, often missing the point of these experiments, which led to further innovation and change, such as Sir Barry Jackson's modern-dress productions in the 1920's. The use of modern dress was in a way a return to the earlier practice, from Shakespeare's time through the eighteenth century, a practice which had long since been forgotten in the nineteenth century's quest for archeological authenticity.[3]

From this superficial and brief survey it should be evident that there are many ways to design sets and costumes for a Shakespeare play and no single 'right' way. But some ways may be more appropriate and effective than others, given the audience, the circumstances, and the particular play. Though it might be argued that modern-dress productions are more 'Shakespearean' than historically costumed ones, there are obvious objections to this position: not only do the plays involve awkward references to such things as doublet and hose (comfortably familiar to an Elizabethan audience), but the lack of an unbroken tradition of contemporary costuming has made it impossible to not look on Shakespeare in modern dress as deliberately unconventional. When some period between Shakespeare's and ours is chosen, or some location far from either Shakespeare's England or the country in which the events supposedly occur is selected, the thoughtful theatregoer will question the rationale for such transpositions and may need some criteria for judging their appropriateness.

What rationales are available for these different designs? Are they all the same, or do they vary from one specific production to another? One rationale is that by changing the locale or time period of the play the production will appear fresher and more relevant to present audiences. Another is that the changes will help uncover hitherto undiscovered or unsuspected aspects of the plays as the company gets away from tradition-bound ways of viewing and, hence, performing them.[4] To a considerable extent these rationales hold up. I can recall, for example, attending a performance years ago of *A Midsummer Night's Dream* at the Cambridge Arts Theatre staged by a troupe from Howard Payne College in the United States. It was advertised as done in 'Texas Western style', appropriately enough as the college was in Texas. Like many others, I expected a burlesque performance but was surprised and delighted to see how well the cowboy and Indian motif worked – the Athenians were cowboys and the fairies Indians – and how the players brought the play, through this unusual perspective, newly to life.

That was in 1959. A decade later Peter Brook took the same play and transformed it utterly in what is now regarded as a landmark production. The squash court set, the actors as acrobats, the doubling of Theseus and Hippolyta with Oberon and Titania, and other innovations were all designed to destroy at a blow the nineteenth-century staging of the *Dream*, complete with Mendelssohn's music and a literal forest growing from the boards. Brook's production was of course more radical than the less ambitious but still effective 'Texas Western' production by Howard Payne College. Both had essentially the same purpose: to awaken our sensibilities to aspects of the play that years of traditional staging had obscured or dulled. The new, untraditional settings not only forced both actors and audience to look at the play afresh, but compelled them to listen more closely to the language, to pay better attention to the verse and prose in order to discover how and if they worked in the new frameworks the productions provided. Regarding his squash court set, Brook said that it would 'emphasize every sound, reveal every movement and give every freedom'. Its bright lighting, moreover, would provide 'a white daylight magic'.[5] Indeed, the circus atmosphere and tricks were an attempt to translate the fairy magic of the original into contemporary equivalents. Purists, of course, found Brook's staging outrageous,[6] and a decade and a half later many have still not forgiven him, though he has had his imitators. Ron Daniels of the Royal Shakespeare Company felt compelled in 1981 to stage the play in a still different fashion – using extra-large puppets as his fairies, manipulated on stage by unobtrusive actors – partly in reaction to (if not against) Brook's production, which has remained indelibly fixed in the minds of many theatregoers, especially in Britain. He retained the doubling of Theseus and Hippolyta, but in other respects the set design was vastly different, literally a throwback to Victorian settings and, in the opening scene in Athens, Victorian attitudes. Daniels was struggling with two traditions, the one old and venerable, the other

[23]

new and radical, and apparently trying to find a middle ground between them while at the same time making a statement of his own.[7] For in his view, the characters are so flagrantly manipulated by those in power that he brought puppets on stage to emphasize the fact to the audience.[8]

Directors and designers (who typically work together in these matters) may, of course, get carried away with their own inspirations. In the process of staging a new production they can (and sometimes do) destroy vital or essential aspects of the play they are presenting. This was clearly the situation when the RSC recently restaged *The Merchant of Venice*, directed by John Caird and designed by Ultz. Three immense caskets, raised or lowered by special levering machines, remained constantly on stage, dominating the set and threatening at any moment to topple off their platforms – directly onto the heads of actors or audience. (When I asked one of the leading actors in the production why the designer had used those cumbersome and treacherous machines, he could only answer that Ultz rather liked them!) And Adrian Noble, it seems, has an affinity to water, as in his productions of *King Lear* and *As You Like It*, which featured what the company fondly referred to as the wading pond at the front edge of the stage. *Julius Caesar* is often played in the costume and setting of fascist Italy, presumably because of the striking resemblances between the two eras, separated though they were by millennia. In some productions, the actor playing Caesar has even adopted the attitudes and stance of Mussolini, as in the BBC television production, thus further emphasizing the connection.

Excesses apart, unusual set designs for the plays – specifically, transpositions of time and place – raise important questions. For example, how far can – or should – a designer go to infuse new life into a play, or revive its old life? Where does legitimate transposition of time and place end and frank adaptation begin? What's wrong with conventional staging in Elizabethan costume anyway? Without resorting to 'museum Shakespeare', can't we have a reasonable approximation of what Shakespeare's audiences saw (and heard) without losing touch with issues or ideas of contemporary relevance?

Recognizing the important differences between proscenium and open stages that perforce influence set design, Peter Brook has argued vigorously against any set that would 'confine the audience to a single attitude and a single interpretation'. The plays being so rich in ambiguity, the director and designer's job is to explore the truths within the ambiguity, not to 'use' the play for some particular –

personal or political or social – interpretation, which makes the play 'a vehicle for exploitation'. For Brook, 'any complete and consistent set of historical costumes is a fantastic imposition' that 'forces the play in certain directions' or places it in a strait-jacket.' You cannot enter into a play if part of you is squashed into [a] footnoting attitude,' he maintains, and concludes: 'To put it very simply: the trap is to make statements and to make illustrations.'[9]

These are very powerful arguments, but interestingly most of the examples Brook gives are from the tragedies. Fifteen years ago, the Regency *Hamlet* with Richard Chamberlain as the Prince focused successfully on certain aspects of the play while it sacrificed others. Emphasizing the romantic, passionate nature of Hamlet, it lost some of the thoughtfulness and melancholy contemplation that make his character an archetype of the divided self. Consider also the striking differences between Brook's own stage production of *King Lear* and the more realistic, historical setting for his film version. The trade-offs, as Ralph Berry remarks, must be reckoned, especially when modern sets are used: 'The danger is always that an immediate point can be made vividly and tellingly, but that it relies on a set of assumptions about our own society that the remainder of the text cannot sustain.'[10] On the whole, as Berry says, modernization or adaptation works better for the comedies than for the tragedies; in the comedies gains achieved through modernizing tend to outweigh losses. Why this should be so is by no means clear: it may be that in comedy spectacle is less distracting and fanciful design, or outright fantasy, is more easily accepted, as Thomas Clayton has suggested.[11] Or perhaps seeing our own society (or one we are close to) mirrored in the follies of Shakespeare's comedies is more acceptable than seeing it in the tragedies, where we require a less specific, more 'timeless' setting – a setting, that is, which helps the play's essential reality to re-emerge, unobstructed and unimpeded by irrelevant or unnecessary topicality.[12]

Whatever the case, sharp lines of demarcation between tragedies and comedies and their settings need not be drawn. Moreover, one of the important gains in changing settings has not been often enough stressed, that is, the advantage in replacing literalistic attitudes toward the plays and their interpretation with more flexible and versatile ones. While altering time-periods may require some adjustments in the text, the changes may not have to be substantial. Certainly, it is gratifying to see directors willing to credit audiences with more nimble imaginations than heretofore, forging another link (I think it is fair to say) between Shakespeare's audiences and ourselves. Thus, Peter Hall bravely mixed contemporary and traditional costumes in the National Theatre production of *Coriolanus*. If there was some slight dissonance in viewing Cominius or Coriolanus now in three-piece suit or blazer and slacks, now in Roman helmet and breastplate with sword and buckler, it mattered little in the overall effect the powerful performances produced. It seems we can do without strict historical verisimilitude or consistency, thanks in part to the relaxing of theatrical conventions and of the historicity nineteenth-century productions promoted. The stage set for Hall's *Coriolanus* was itself a model of simplicity and versatility. Borrowing the sand pit from his earlier RSC production of *Troilus and Cressida*, Hall encircled it with a concrete runway and placed two huge doors or gates upstage with several tiers of benches on either side from which the audience/crowd could descend as needed. By using other elements of the Olivier Theatre's open stage, such as the configuration of the stalls and the aisles as entrance ways, Hall succeeded in surrounding the action, thereby drawing the audience further into the play. In fact, the physical staging more than the mixed costume design did much to accomplish this end. On the other hand, some spectators found the stage audience and the way they were used to be a distraction.

To return to comedies and the more audacious set designs they tend to evoke: consider two American productions of *Much Ado About Nothing*, a decade apart and quite distinctly staged. First, Joseph Papp's production (1972) directed by A. J. Antoon, mentioned in the previous chapter. Recall that it was set in a small American town at the turn of the century, or in the period of the Spanish-American War. Apart from making the play more accessible to American audiences, the design of this production revitalized the play much in the way that Howard Payne College did *A Midsummer Night's Dream*. Again, no violence was done to Shakespeare's basic conception – his Messina of the 1590s and middle-America in the 1890s turn out to have much in common! Beatrice, played by Kathleen Widdoes, was a woman of her time, but also outspoken and daring – an early version of feminism quite consistent with Shakespeare's characterization. (Her sneaking a cigarette on the porch and sharing it among her nervous girlfriends was one of several 'modern' touches.) Similarly, Sam Waterston as Captain Benedick, in uniform or out, retained all of the essentials of his role. The greatest liberties were taken with Don John, the comic villain (seen in I.iii shooting at ducks in a pond – and missing), with his cohorts, and with the Keystone Kops who became the Watch. But the liberties were not extreme and they fit nicely into the overall design of the play. The play was a success on Broadway and afterwards on network television.[13]

John Neville-Andrews used quite a different design in 1985 for his Folger Theatre production, the 1930s cruise ship motif. His justification for this setting, as stated in the programme notes, was a curious mixture of the right thing for the wrong reasons. 'The thirties,' he said, 'was an extremely joyous, optimistic and romantic era, and I saw it as reflecting the spirit of the play. The personality of the period can be evoked by recalling such songs, events and milestones as' – he goes on to list a great many, including Bobby Jones's 'Grand Slam' achievement in world golf, the discovery of Vitamin D, the establishment of the forty-hour work week, 'I Got Rhythm', nylon stockings, and the launching of the S. S. *Queen Elizabeth*! Now anyone who lived through the Depression years will recall that it was far from a 'joyous' or 'optimistic' era, however romantic or even idealistic in some respects it may have been. People sought escape from their troubles and found in the field of entertainment a wonderful vehicle. Technicolor movies (an invention not on Neville-Andrews's list) were one such outlet, Broadway shows another, and, for the very rich, there were Mediterranean cruises. The milieu of *Much Ado*, the tight uppercrust society of Messina, lends itself quite well to the wealthy voyagers on this early version of the 'Love Boat', just as it did to the small 1890s middle-American town in Papp's production.[14] Shakespeare's Watch were easily transformed into the ship's crew, and Don John as a mafia-type villain was comical in ways essentially consistent with the text (except, possibly, for his heavy New York accent). Designer William Barclay performed a minor miracle in converting the Folger's tiny apron stage into the deck of an ocean liner, a bit crowded at times, but not excessively. The pianist playing Cole Porter melodies in the ship's lounge was an excellent period touch. Where Neville-Andrews went wrong was to introduce (in the hope of some additional – but quite unnecessary – comedy) an 'Unlisted Passenger' aboard the S. S. *Messina*, a stowaway whose mysterious presence was explained only at the very end when, as an undercover agent for the F.B.I., she apprehended Don John!

Neville-Andrews's setting for *Much Ado* (like the Spanish-American War setting for the play in Papp's production) helped to bring out the timeless quality of Shakespeare's comedy – not by removing all suggestions of time and place but, on the contrary, by being very specific about both. The ideas and attitudes of sixteenth-century Sicily (or England) appear not very far removed, after all, from those of more recent periods, though still distanced from us sufficiently to afford an objective judgement that is vital for comedy. What then should we make of Michael Rudman's National Theatre production of *Measure for Measure* at the Lyttleton Theatre in 1981? Instead of Shakespeare's Vienna, the setting was a contemporary Caribbean banana republic, complete with palm trees and calypso music. The nearly all-black cast was an interesting innovation for this particular play, although not an unprecedented novelty. The Duke was perhaps too laid-back even for Shakespeare's Vincentio, but Angelo and Isabella were the puritanical characters of the original. Little of the text was cut, and some songs and music were added.

Although the basic conception for this *Measure for Measure* was plausible and worked fairly well, it was not a smashing success. Why not? Probably because, in this instance, the conception was not exploited fully enough. The taste for a calypso *Measure for Measure* was merely whetted, hardly satisfied. One could see the potential for a rollicking, a-moral ambience – the underworld of Vienna transformed to a sunnier and more exuberant Caribbean milieu reflecting an environment more radically informed by a zest for life than the original one. What was presented, however, was – given the conception and its potential – much too restrained, or perhaps underdeveloped. In other words, the transposition was not complete, being at once too close and too far from Shakespeare's original. The equivalences in setting, characterization, and time were not worked out thoroughly, so that the production still looked like a transplant, not an indigenous flowering.[15] Is that the real danger in transposing Shakespeare's settings? If the designer and director do not go far enough to make the transposition appear not to be what it is – a transposition – then what are the chances of success? To convey credibility, must the production seem to be original to the time and place, even though we know it is not?

Finally, what about the history plays, which would seem, quite rightly, to resist alterations of time and place? It should not surprise us, however, that some interesting attempts to do just this have been made. Not every aspect of *Richard II* quite fits a Marxist interpretation, but when in 1981 the Young Vic staged the play in the costume of revolutionary Russia, with Bolingbroke looking very much like Lenin and Richard like the hapless Czar, a certain point was made and a relevance established that connected the power politics of the fourteenth century (as seen by Shakespeare) with the power struggles among the Russians.

A more radical transposition was tried in the summer of 1984 by the Shakespeare Festival at Santa Cruz, California, where Michael Edwards directed *Henry IV, Part One*, in modern dress. Falstaff was an ageing Hell's Angel, and Prince Hal's cronies were part of a gang of bikers (Hal's initial entrance was, appropriately then, upon a dirt bike). Budweiser replaced sack, machine guns substituted for swords, and a strong anti-war motif (redolent of Vietnam protest marches and, more recently, anti-Contra demonstrations) suffused the whole. Henry IV became a tycoon and later a five-star general, with Westmoreland as a presidential aide and Blunt a Pentagon general. The emphasis upon 'political wheeling-dealing', as Alan Dessen describes the main plot scenes, made a certain kind of sense in a presidential election year in the United States, given the candidates and the issues. Some aspects of Shakespeare's original were of course sacrificed, such as the image of the crown and other emblems of late medieval royalty, but the gains that the production achieved seemed to make the trade-offs worthwhile.[16]

From here it is but a step to more or less complete adaptation, as in *Your Own Thing* (from *Twelfth Night*) or, at the extreme end, a Shogun *Macbeth* or a Kabuki *Othello*, both of which have recently graced American stages. Much can be said that is instructive, as Ruby Cohn has done in her book, *Shakespearean Offshoots*. In those cases Shakespeare's plays as we know them almost entirely vanish from sight, transformed into new images, often rich and strange ones. But these are not our concern here.

As we have seen, the visual aspects of a production can help freshen our perspectives on Shakespeare's work, emphasizing relevance in startling and original ways that do not necessarily conflict with the essentials of the drama. Or they can so distract or distort that we find the connections between Shakespeare's original and the current production too distant – so far removed, in fact, that

[29]

we are compelled to reject the production altogether. A design that works for rather than against a play requires taste, imagination, and wit along with a deep understanding of – and respect for – the text. For that is always what we come back to in the end, remembering that in Shakespeare's 'wooden O', the Globe, sets were unheard of (in the modern sense); so were elaborate lighting and many of the other advantages of contemporary technology. Modern set designers need hardly eschew these advantages – Shakespeare surely would not have – but they must be careful not to let them become the controlling aspect of a production. For then we are indeed, as Ralph Berry has warned, in 'designers' theatre' and no longer in Shakespeare's, where language and action are – and should remain – the primary elements of his dramatic art.

CHAPTER III

Finding the characters

When near the end of Act II in *Henry IV, Part One* Falstaff concludes his long and moving appeal on behalf of all he represents – 'banish plump Jack, and banish all the world' – Prince Hal has four words in reply: 'I do, I will.' The pressure on these four words is enormous, for behind them lies the long, rollicking relationship between the fat knight and the madcap young man, a relationship founded partly on Falstaff's dependence on the Prince but more on the good times – the adventures, the sallies of wit, the camaraderie – they have enjoyed together. How then should Hal pronounce these terrible and terrifying words? Quietly, almost *sotto voce*? jokingly, in keeping with play extempore they have been acting out? tendentiously, deliberately trying to puncture the vain bubble the old man has been blowing? nervously, with awareness of the expectations others have of him and his position as Prince of Wales? Much will depend upon how the actor conceives the role, the discoveries he has made about the character he is enacting on the stage, and the relationship that has developed between Falstaff and Hal in the particular production of the play.[1]

Finding the character is perhaps the most difficult problem an actor has to solve in approaching any important role, though even minor roles raise similar questions. (How does the Sheriff, who enters soon afterward, address the Prince? Is he officious or obsequious? or something in between?) The problem is no less acute for the audience, which must try to understand the main thrust of the character but also the subtleties of behavior, the nuances and innuendoes that the actor may discover in the role and try to bring out in the performance. Complicating everything, of course, is that the roles have been played before – in the major plays, very often over the years, stretching back for centuries in sometimes well-documented and celebrated productions. Thus Antony Sher in 1984 had to find a different Richard III, playing against the character as Olivier had portrayed him in the famous film that has had widespread and repeated showings since its premiere in 1955. Essentially, of course, their Richards are the same: inordinately ambitious, cunning, and vicious, with enough wit and power also to make them attractive. How else can Richard win Lady Anne, even as she mourns over her father-in-law's casket? But no one seeing both performances would for a moment mistake Sher's Richard for Olivier's – and this is not a matter solely of the wicked crutches Sher used in his performance. Where Olivier was awesome and masterful – for all his withered arm and humped back – Sher was small and spidery, swiftly entrapping his victims who, caught like any fly in a web, found themselves suddenly powerless before him.

Are both Richards valid? How are we to choose between them? Need we choose, or can we see in these distinctive representations of a major character alternative ways of playing the role, both compelling, both in their way authentic? Does one interpretation cancel out the other or, on the contrary, do they complement each other in ways that enlarge the part in our imagination, opening up new possibilities for understanding the complexity that neither actor has invented for the role but has found in it instead?[2] And what is true for *Richard III* is true for Shakespeare's other plays.[3] If there is no one right way of portraying a character, no single definitive representation, how can we determine acceptable from unacceptable, because distorted, representations? In what do the essentials of the character lie? And how can we know what they are?

We must begin, like the actors, with a close reading of the text along with our own experience of reality, of other people and ourselves in action and reflection. The clues in the text are abundant, sometimes even contradictory. Shakespearean characters need not be absolutely consistent any more than we expect people we know to be consistent in everything they do or say. Characters, like people, have their moods and moments. As J. L. Styan reminds us in his discussion of Helena in *All's Well That Ends Well*, ambiguity can be an important – and eminently useful – attribute of a character that an actor can and should develop.[4] But underlying the ambiguities, the contradictions and the inconsistencies, are discernible attitudes and ideas that motivate behavior, and it is the actor's job – and ours, through him or her – to find these out. Not an easy job, since interpretation is at the heart of the process. Not an impossible one, either. Careful attention and sensitivity are required, along with some understanding of the play and its possibilities.

Fortunately, accounts of how actors have found their roles are available to help us understand the process at its genesis. A recent collection edited by Philip Brockbank, *Players of Shakespeare* (Cambridge, 1985), includes a dozen highly informative and illuminating essays by members of the Royal Shakespeare Company on a variety of roles, from Patrick Stewart on Shylock to Michael Pennington on Hamlet, and from Sinead Cusack on Portia to Gemma Jones on Hermione. Each account is different, as the actors grappled in different ways to understand the characters they were chosen to portray. A single constant, however, runs throughout: reading and rereading and again rereading the text. Only there do the actors find the essential clues to an understanding of their roles.

Consider, for example, David Suchet's dilemma in preparing to play Caliban in *The Tempest*. He had never acted the role before and had only once seen it performed, many years earlier. After reading over the text and discussing the part with the director, Clifford Williams, Suchet had no clear idea of what Caliban looked like, though he had some sense of what his motivations were. He went to the Shakespeare Centre Library in Stratford to do a little research and discovered that Caliban had been played as a fish, a dog, a lizard, a monkey, a tortoise, and so on. Dissatisfied with all of these interpretations, he hunted through the text for indications of what Shakespeare intended for Caliban and discovered that, although he doubtless smelled fishy and may have been somewhat unusual in appearance, he was certainly human in shape. One of the clues is that Miranda includes him among the only two men she has ever seen before meeting Ferdinand (I.ii.446). Another is Prospero's narrative on what the island was like when he and his daughter first landed there (I.ii.281-6). As Suchet says, the punctuation of Prospero's lines is important, even as they were first printed in the Folio:

> Then was this Island
> (Saue for the Son, that she did littour heere,
> A frekelld whelpe, hag-borne) not honour'd with
> A humane shape.

Stage tradition had obviously gone wrong in making Caliban a fantastical, misshapen creature, depending on Trinculo's and Stephano's initial impressions of him as a 'monster' rather than on the more reliable testimony from other characters in the play. As Suchet's further research uncovered, Shakespeare probably had in mind for the part some kind of 'native', a cross between an American Indian and an African black, perhaps. In his representation of Caliban and the makeup he accordingly used, Suchet found this notion of the role much more useful than any his predecessors had adopted. His performance was a striking success.

Motivation – what makes a character behave as he or she does – gets closer to the heart of the problem, and here actors must penetrate to the essentials of their roles. Typically, actors fret a good deal about this, searching the text for clues but examining also their own experiences and those of their friends or fellow actors for indications, hints, parallels. Often, they are frightened when tackling a new role, especially when invited to play Shakespeare, and the fear is not altogether a bad thing. It can be a healthy encouragement to explore deeply and carefully both the role and oneself – finally, oneself in the role.

This was Gemma Jones's situation when she agreed to play Hermione in *The Winter's Tale*. She says she reacted initially like 'a nervous novice'.[5] Although she had read and reread the text several times, she still lacked an 'instantly clear vision' of the role. She understood the words Hermione speaks, but the motives remained obscure:

> I suspect that she has no ulterior motive and that she is indeed 'The Good Queen', 'Continent, chaste and true'. I am reluctant to accept it. I resist 'good'. Why? Why do I suppose that good must therefore be insipid, sweet, weak and uninteresting? I admit that my objection to 'good' is partly my egotistical desire for me as an actress to impress; to act devious, clever, complicated and interesting. Yet surely good need not be passive. She can still be full-blooded, womanly, wise and humorous. My internal dialogues are so devious, clever, complicated and interesting that more often than not I forget where I started and can't find the way out.[6]

[34]

Conversations with Patrick Stewart who plays Leontes and Ray Jewers who plays Polixenes prove helpful. All three are parents and partners of parents. They discuss pregnancy: 'I admit to a state of introverted self-satisfaction which allowed for no intrusion and blinded me to needs outside myself, while the men acknowledge certain feelings of impotent isolation and rejection.'[7] Here lies a clue to Hermione's behaviour in Act I, her apparent blindness to what Leontes is feeling. Moreover, her maternity and the child she already has (Mamillius) may prompt in her a love for both her husband and his friend that is entirely chaste and highly compassionate.

But discussions, however 'interesting, entertaining and enlightening', don't solve the main problem, which remains, as Hamlet says, how 'to suit the action to the word'. Rehearsals help. Different approaches are tried, rejected, sorted out. Gradually, Jones moves into the role, recognizing that while she must endow Hermione with her own personality and her own complexities – the sum of her experiences as a woman – a good deal of self-discipline is also necessary. The role is particularly difficult because there are only four scenes in which Hermione appears, scarcely enough to build upon, but it must be done. The 'Good Queen' of Acts I and II has her climactic moments in the Trial Scene of Act III. The 'intellectual agility' of her speeches in the first scene gives way to the greater fluidity and simplicity of her speeches here. But even these are not without their underlying complexities, which must be 'excavated, minutely examined and then reassembled to their original simplicity'. The motive force now is Hermione's inherent innocence and truth, which do not require special pleading or proof. The words must be allowed to flow into one another unencumbered with tricks or sophistication. It works. Only the Statue Scene remains – a long way off in Act V, scene iii, with different problems to be solved.

Directors can be and often are helpful to actors trying to find their way into roles, but even their usefulness is limited. In *Playing Shakespeare* John Barton discusses the productions of *The Merchant of Venice* he directed, the first one with Patrick Stewart as Shylock, the second shortly afterwards with David Suchet. The overall conceptions for the productions were similar, if not identical, but the Shylocks were very different, even though Barton had told each of the actors much the same things. 'Basically I gave Patrick and David the same directions and made the same points, both in detail and in general. Yet. . . the result was utterly different and individual.'[8] The reasons are not hard to seek: Barton was dealing with two very competent but very individual actors, with different experiences, personalities, imaginations. Moreover, the role itself is filled with contradictions and inconsistencies, ambiguities that allow for various interpretations, no single one of them 'right', but any of them justified by a careful reading of the text and its interpretation.[9]

To test this approach, consider the question of Shylock's Jewishness. How 'Jewish' is he, that is, how much should the fact of his Jewishness be emphasized in performance? Stewart argues that Shylock's Jewishness is irrelevant, a distraction when emphasized; he is essentially an alien, an outsider, who happens to be a Jew. In that way you can get to the universality of the character and overcome the danger of his becoming 'only a symbol'. Suchet cannot agree. For him, Shylock is an outsider because he is a Jew. 'The Jewish element in the play is unavoidable and very important.'[10] Although both actors concur that the play is not anti-Semitic (despite the anti-Semitism it contains), they recognize that in the latter part of the twentieth century this aspect cannot be ignored; it must be reckoned with. That each of them did so in quite different ways leading to quite different performances indicates the richness of the character and the possibilities for interpretation. Stewart spoke in a way that was highly cultured and refined to stress Shylock's urge – outsider that he was – to assimilate more completely into the society which attempted to exclude him. Suchet adopted a slight accent to suggest his foreignness. Either way, Shylock stood apart from his fellows, but both the causes and the effects were radically different, and neither of them was 'wrong'.[11] Suchet may have been closer to the historical background (Shylock was a comic villain in the original conception of the role), whereas Stewart was closer to the character as a contemporary audience might relate to him. But neither strayed from the text in his interpretation.

Often, it is not just a matter of an actor's finding a way into a role alone, but the interaction of two or more actors working closely together to establish a relationship that their roles demand. Edgar interacts differently with many of the major characters in *King Lear*, according to the situations he finds himself in.[12] One major interaction involves the scenes in Act III where we first see him as the madman, Poor Tom of Bedlam. Lear is out on the heath, his wits now definitely turning – by the end of III.vi he will be out of them altogether – the result of the cruelty of his two unnatural daughters. In contrast, Edgar as Poor Tom puts on an assumed madness. How do his pretended madness and Lear's real one affect each other? More to the point, how do they affect us, the audience and witnesses to their scenes together? Citing Edgar's soliloquy in II.iii as evidence, Michael Goldman argues that Edgar's disguise is designed to be as repulsive as possible: 'He is the kind of beggar who *enforces* charity – so repellent, nasty, and noisy that you pay him to go away.'[13] But he is seldom portrayed this way, because it complicates further the tremendous problems the actor playing Lear already has. For Lear has to get through not only these difficult scenes in Act III, but the extremely trying ones in Acts IV and V. 'Full loathsomeness for Edgar means added impossibilities for Lear.'

The Fool in *King Lear* is more fortunate. Having endured so much with Lear already, he ends his role in III.vi. But how should his 'follies' play against his master's? What effect do they have on the old king? Do his songs and riddles provide any relief for Lear's sufferings, evoking the momentary release that laughter brings? Or do they carry barbs that aggravate wounds he already feels? Can they do both simultaneously? (Antony Sher's portrayal seemed to accomplish this feat in the RSC's 1982 production of the play, directed by Adrian Noble and heavily influenced by Samuel Beckett.) The Fool enters in Act I, scene iv, after Cordelia's banishment and disappears before she returns in Act IV. Both try to minister to Lear in their different ways. Though they never appear together, what is their implied relationship, and how is the audience meant to keep it in mind? That the Fool loved Cordelia is clear from Act I, when the Knight responds to Lear's repeated questions regarding the Fool's whereabouts: 'Since my young lady's going into France, sir, the Fool hath much pin'd away' (I.iv.73-74). Although Cordelia and the Fool minister to Lear in different ways, their dramatic functions are closely related: is it conceivable that the two roles are really one? Could the boy actor who played Cordelia also have played the Fool? If that is unlikely, could Robert Armin in Shakespeare's company have played both roles?[14] An actress might be able to enact both parts,[15] but is this too easy a way to identify the roles and their relationship? Is it better, rather, to do so by stressing the tenderness and love that underlie both Cordelia's harsh candour in scene one and the Fool's taunts in Acts I and II?[16]

Questions like these derive directly from our understanding of roles and interrelationships vital to performance. In *Macbeth* the leading roles of Macbeth and Lady Macbeth depend on each other for their proper realization on the stage, especially in the first two acts, until Macbeth has accomplished the assassination of King Duncan. But bringing him to that momentous deed is an essential function of Lady Macbeth. How does she do it? What kind of woman does the text present? That is the question that must be asked first, because the kind of woman she is influences the way she behaves toward Macbeth and he toward her. As Carol Carlisle has shown, actors and actresses have divided into two schools of thought concerning Macbeth's wife. 'Is she a "fiend" – a terrible though possibly magnificent incarnation of evil? Or is she a recognizable, perhaps even a sympathetic, human being?'[17] The polarity of opinions divides again into questions about her 'masculinity' or 'femininity': Is she an imposing, dominating figure; 'a wily temptress'; a charming, even seductive wife; a devoted helpmate; some combination of these types? While her ambition is more urgent than Macbeth's in the early scenes of the play – she forces him to close the gap between 'I dare not' and 'I would' – what fuels her ambition? What is her source of power – not only over him, but within herself? Before an actress can assay the role of Lady Macbeth, she must answer these questions, at least in a preliminary way. More definite answers – for the particular production, at any rate – will follow after rehearsals have begun and even after the show has opened.

For experience has repeatedly shown that productions of Shakespeare's plays (and those of many other playwrights) are seldom 'frozen' by the end of dress rehearsals. They continue to evolve, as actors and actresses discover a greater range of possible interpretations than they at first realized. Audience response is important, too, and will affect a performance on any given occasion. In the course of playing, the actors will try to establish rapport with their audience, so that an emphasis that worked for one audience may have to be adjusted, if ever so slightly, to fit the attitudes and responses of another. Finding the character that a particular audience can respond to actively and fully then becomes the excitement of 'live theatre' for the cast and, although it may be much more unaware of the process, for the audience, too.

[38]

CHAPTER IV

Finding the subtext

Part of the hard job of finding the character is finding the 'subtext' for the character.[1] This term, as it has come into increasingly wide use, has become subject to loosening definition. It may be useful, therefore, to go back to its origin in the work of Constantin Stanislavski, the great actor, director, and producer of the Moscow Art Theatre, whose influence has extended well beyond the Russian stage and is still a vital force today.

The term first appeared in English in Elizabeth Hapgood's translation of *Building a Character* (New York, 1949), the sequel to Stanislavski's *An Actor Prepares* (New York, 1936), also translated by Hapgood. But the essential concept is strongly implied in the earlier book, particularly where Stanislavski, in the persona of the Director, Tortsov, speaks about the inner feelings and thoughts an actor must have to produce effective, honest representation. For example, in the chapter on 'Adaptation', Tortsov says to his students:

> Do you suppose that words can exhaust all the nicest shadings of the emotion you experience? No! When we are communing with one another words do not suffice. If we want to put life into them, we must produce feelings. They fill out the blanks left by words, they finish what has been left unsaid. (p. 212)

If text is the essential thing in a Shakespearean – or any other – play, it is not the only thing, and actors must endeavor to find those unwritten, or unspoken, indications – those feelings, ideas, thoughts – that help make characters what they are, or make them behave in certain ways.

This is why subtext is important. It is directly related both to the script the actor is performing and to the actor's inner creative life – the ability to infuse life into a script, or rather breathe life from it. For subtext 'lies behind and beneath the actual words of a part' (*Building a Character*, p. 107). It is

> the manifest, the inwardly felt expression of a human being in a part, which flows uninterruptedly beneath the words of the text, giving them life and a basis for existing. The subtext is a web of innumerable, varied patterns inside a play and a part, woven from 'magic ifs', given circumstances, all sorts of figments of imagination, inner movements, objects of attention, smaller and greater truths and a belief in them, adaptations, adjustments and other similar elements. It is the subtext that makes us say the words we do in a play. (p. 108)

Stanislavski goes on to say that 'only when our feelings reach down into the subtextual stream that the "through line of action" of a play or part comes into being'. And it is this 'through line of action' that to him is all-important in successful theatrical representation; without it a play exists only in fragments, broken bits and pieces that, however brilliantly contrived individually, fail to cohere into the unified whole without which no play or part can be called successful.

Later on we shall return to the 'through line of action' and to subtext as they relate to the overall interpretation of a play. Here, let the focus remain, as in the previous chapter, on subtext as it concerns the full development of character and the interaction between characters. For Stanislavski, as for most actors and directors, the printed text is no more a finished product than a musical score is. Both require performance for full realization, and performance means interpretation, whether in actual performance on stage or in the 'theatre of the mind'. Words need to be spoken, to be heard; characters need to act, to move about; feelings must be aroused, questions raised, thinking stimulated. Only then does a play come alive, and finding the subtext is a very large part of each actor's task in bringing the play to life.

Although Stanislavski may have invented the term, the idea of subtext, the undercurrent of thought and feeling with which the text is charged, was familiar to actors before him. In *Shakespeare's*

[40]

Plays in Performance (London, 1966), John Russell Brown cites Macready's definition of the art of acting, as recalled by another great nineteenth-century actor, Henry Irving:

> What is the art of acting? . . . It is the art of embodying the poet's creations, of giving them flesh and blood, of making the figures which appeal to your mind's eye in the printed drama live before you on the stage. 'To fathom the depths of character, to trace its latent motives, to feel its finest quiverings of emotion, to comprehend the thoughts that are hidden under the words, and thus possess one's self of the actual mind of the individual man' – such was Macready's definition of the player's art. (p. 65)

Without question, the actor's responsibility here is enormous: how indeed is he or she to trace the latent motives of a character, to comprehend the thoughts hidden under the words, and in these ways to fathom the depths that dialogue only partly reveals? How can actors know any representation is what the playwright originally conceived? Of course, neither they nor anyone can know this, for much of it lies beneath the conscious level both in its original creation and in its later embodiment. The only guide is, once more, the text and the various clues and suggestions it provides.

That Shakespeare was aware of a reality underlying the spoken words of his dialogue is clear from a number of passages, such as those that John Russell Brown quotes from *A Midsummer Night's Dream*, *Hamlet*, and other plays.[2] In his first speech to his mother, for example, Hamlet pointedly refers to external trappings of mourning that scarcely reflect the real feelings he has about his father's death (and at the same time indirectly hurls an accusation at Gertrude about her own behaviour). Disguise is another means that Shakespeare uses to indicate a disparity between spoken words and their underlying reality, according to Brown. Puns and quibbles function in this way, too, as Hamlet's opening lines to Claudius reveal (see below, p. 58).

Often the imagery that a character uses offers an important clue to the subtextual reality that can provide a major motivation for attitude and behaviour. Ambition has usually been cited as the main reason for Macbeth's murder of Duncan, but the subtextual reality shows that his situation is far more complex. Fear is an important part of his being, both the fear of retribution 'here, upon this bank and shoal of time' (I.vii.6) and the fear of seeming unmanly to his wife. His essential humanity is revealed not only by Lady Macbeth's concern that he is 'too full of the milk of human kindness', but by the imagery Macbeth uses of the 'naked new-born babe, / Striding the blast' or the vision of heaven's cherubin blowing his 'horrid deed' in every eye, 'That tears shall drown the wind' (I.vii.21-24). Like Lady Macbeth, he too must somehow eradicate from his being all sense of feeling and remorse, the 'great bond' that unites him to humanity, if he is to go forward in his plan to seize the crown the nearest way and hold on to it. The extreme effort it takes to do this is a vital part of his nature, and the actor playing the role must derive from subtextual reality the energy, thought, and feeling to realize the character fully. If he is successful, Macbeth's later despair and his feeling of being utterly worn out by the end can become overwhelmingly effective. Apparently, this is how Nicol Williamson conceived the role in the BBC-TV production of *Macbeth*.

Derek Jacobi's performance of Prospero in the Royal Shakespeare Company's production of *The Tempest* (1982) was informed by a refreshing interpretation of the part. Averse to playing Prospero as an old man, Jacobi saw him as someone in his forties (the actor's own age), plausible enough from the text. As a basic part of his subtext, Jacobi found Prospero not only younger, but angrier than he is usually played. Still smouldering with resentment after many years of exile on his enchanted island, Prospero awaits his opportunity, finally at hand, to take revenge on the malefactors who forced him from his dukedom and set him adrift in a 'rotten carcass of a butt' with his only child, Miranda. This subtext was suggested by the dialogue with Ariel at the beginning of the last act. By this time, Prospero's plot has worked exceedingly well. He has all his enemies completely in his power – Alonzo, Sebastian, Antonio – and Caliban and his motley crew have also been taken care of. Ariel has carried out his instructions perfectly, and the magician's project 'gathers to a head'. Ariel informs his master that Alonzo and his followers are all prisoners confined together

> In the lime-grove which weather-fends your cell;
> They cannot boudge till your release. The King,
> His brother, and yours, abide all three distracted,
> And the remainder mourning over them,
> Brimful of sorrow and dismay; but chiefly
> Him that you term'd, sir, 'The good old Lord Gonzalo',
> His tears run down his beard like winter's drops
> From eaves of reeds. Your charm so strongly works 'em
> That if you now beheld them, your affections
> Would become tender. (10-19)

Prospero – surprised at Ariel's reaction to their plight (he is not human and Prospero is) – takes Ariel's point and making an effort to do so (in Jacobi's portrayal) resolves to be compassionate:

> Hast thou, which art but air, a touch, a feeling
> Of their afflictions, and shall not myself,
> One of their kind, that relish all as sharply
> Passion as they, be kindlier mov'd than thou art?
> Though with their high wrongs I am strook to th' quick,
> Yet, with my nobler reason, 'gainst my fury
> Do I take part. The rarer action is
> In virtue than in vengeance. They being penitent,
> The sole drift of my purpose doth extend
> Not a frown further. (21-30)

Prospero's compassion works, and the malefactors are penitent; certainly Alonzo is and accordingly is reunited with his son, now betrothed to Miranda, discovered with him chastely playing chess. About Antonio and Sebastian we are less sure; the text suggests they may be recalcitrant, everything they have experienced notwithstanding. The subtexts for these roles welcome investigation, too.[3]

Without doubt Falstaff is one of the greatest dramatic characters ever created – and one of the most difficult to perform. The complexities inherent in the character are profound, as Anthony Quayle, who has created the role on both stage and television, has commented. One of the most fully alive personages in all Shakespearean drama, Falstaff is aware of his own shortcomings and failings as well as those of others on whom, parasite that he is, he preys. Genuinely fond of Prince Hal, he uses him shamelessly, but he also feels hurt, Quayle insists, in their wit-combats when Hal scores against him by calling him a 'Manningtree ox' or a ton of lard, because the points Hal makes are accurate. Falstaff has tremendous wit and skill, which he demonstrates superbly, for instance, in the Boar's Head Tavern scenes; he can be outrageous and funny and extremely good company. But somewhere inside him, according to Quayle, 'there's a terrible grief. . . an immense hurt'.[4] Perhaps that accounts for the dark side of Falstaff, which Quayle and others have recognized.[5] Witty and warm and full of life, he is also worldly-wise and cynical. His behaviour at Shrewsbury Field brings out some of the worst in his character, particularly his treatment of the slain Hotspur. 'That's the crucial point where the relationship between Falstaff and Henry falls apart,' Quayle says. 'It's horrible. You mustn't pull your punches if you're playing Falstaff at all. In that sequence he's a rat, a great fat rat.'[6]

Sometimes a subtext will be found not to work and must be discarded, as Laurence Olivier discovered when playing the role of Coriolanus for the second time after a period of eighteen years. In this production, directed by Peter Hall, he tried to find some new secrets about the character, whom he had considered basically a 'a very straightforward, reactionary son of a so-and-so. . . a patrician first and foremost' whose pride is so great that he is 'too proud even to accept praise'.[7] In rehearsal Olivier and Hall experimented with the idea that his inability to accept praise had something to do with the fact that Coriolanus was not really a good soldier, that he was a 'phoney'. But the idea did not work and could not, for if Coriolanus is not an exceptional warrior, who would follow him into battle?

Tyrone Guthrie's conception of Coriolanus is more subtle and psychologically more complex – and perhaps more convincing. He believed the role of Aufidius in the play is crucial and showed how Shakespeare carefully builds that character through the first three acts to the culminating scene in Act IV where Coriolanus, exiled from Rome, meets his former enemy in the Volscian city, Antium. For Guthrie, the scene is nothing less than a love scene, expressing powerfully the positive aspect of the love-hate relationship that has grown between the two antagonists. After a long pause during which the audience cannot tell what effect Coriolanus's speech has had on Aufidius, the Volscian general starts speaking very gently and emotionally. At line 106, when Aufidius expresses his absolute belief in him, Coriolanus at last breaks down in tears, and Aufidius embraces him, like a father his wayward son.[8]

In this interpretation, the subtext is Coriolanus's lack of a father or an older brother whose love is essential as a counterforce to the influence of his dominating mother. It helps explain in more profound psychological terms Coriolanus's betrayal of Rome – not a spoiled child's pique (as in Shakespeare's source, Plutarch), but compensation for rejection by his mother, both his real mother and Rome, his mother country. For in Guthrie's view, Coriolanus feels deeply the rejection by his mother since it was she, against his better judgement, who compelled him to stand for the consulship and confront both the tribunes and the plebians, actions which led directly to his expulsion from Rome. Wounded and homeless, he at last finds shelter in Aufidius, who warmly takes him in. 'The image of the career-rival now presents itself as a possible father or elder brother, something which has always been missing from his life.'[9]

While an examination of the text – both what it reveals and what it conceals – helps to discover possible subtexts for the representation of Shakespeare's characters, how can an audience, sitting in the theatre, find the subtext that an actor is using for the character he or she is presenting? And how can that subtext be verified? Moreover, how can the intelligent spectator judge whether the subtext, once ascertained, is an appropriate or useful one? (It is probably better to avoid judgements like 'right' or 'correct' for the time being.) The best indication of the working subtext is the emphasis, or slant, the actor has adopted. For example, several subtexts are possible for the character of Isabella in *Measure for Measure*. Although the actress in the role will usually indicate which she has chosen very early, its fullest expression may not become manifest until the final scene. There she must react to the Duke's repeated proposal of marriage, and how she responds is the clearest indication of the kind of person the actress conceives Isabella to be. Is she a young woman deeply committed to the religious life, as she appears to be in I.iv.1-5, wishing that the sisters of St. Clare, strict as they are, had even stricter regulations to observe? Or is she a woman sexually repressed, whose devotion to religion is an attempt to sublimate feelings she cannot otherwise express? What exactly does she mean by those terrible words, 'More than our brother is our chastity' (II.iv.185)? In III.i she seems genuinely devoted to her brother and is at first unable to tell him about Angelo's despicable proposition. Tender and considerate, she breaks out into a furious tirade only after Claudio's initial resolve falters and then breaks, as he begs her to save his life.

Doubtless, Isabella has a great deal to learn about herself and about the ways of this world. What she learns, guided mainly by the Duke's interventions from Act III onwards, is partly revealed by her willingness to beg for Angelo's life at the end, believing all the while that her brother is dead at his command. Here she demonstrates that she has learned much about the nature of Christian mercy, especially within the context (which the Duke appears to provide) of unmitigated justice, although her mercy is actually directed as much to the wronged Mariana as to Angelo. But the situation is more complicated than that, and her learning does not stop there. When Claudio enters alive after all and the Duke's schemes are revealed for what they are, Isabella must sort out her conflicting thoughts and emotions. How shall she regard Vincentio now? As a manipulating intruder into other people's lives? As a beneficent ruler trying to promote his subjects' welfare? As a wise teacher or spiritual guide? Or as a meddling old busybody who takes pleasure in his own contrivances?

The answers to these questions of course depend in part on how the Duke is played – what subtext he manifests (again, several are possible) – and Jane Williamson has discussed both his role and Isabella's in an interesting essay.[10] But regardless of how benevolent the Duke is or intends himself to be, Isabella has several choices open to her, which a number of recent stage productions have shown. Up until John Barton's Royal Shakespeare Company production of 1970, Isabella typically joined hands with Vincentio at the end, accepting his proposal of marriage (this is a comedy, after all[11]), and went merrily off with the other happy couples. In point of fact, however, Shakespeare's text does not – either through dialogue or stage direction – give an explicit cue for such an ending. It is left, as John Barton viewed the situation, entirely open, and many other directors have since adopted that view. Hence, Estelle Kohler as Isabella in Barton's production could reasonably choose at the end to remain bewildered and dismayed at the Duke's proposal, even angry and defiant at his presumption.[12] Isabella in Keith Hack's RSC production four years later, according to Ralph Berry, was 'tense and resistant, appeared at the end as an animal trapped in the clutches of a demoniac Duke. Given the pantomime villain confronting her, she could scarcely appear otherwise, and one reviewer saw her progress as a "slow withdrawal into complete horror and implied madness".'[13] Directing at Stratford, Ontario, in 1975, Robin Phillips emphasized the inherent ambiguity of the ending. Martha Henry's Isabella, 'at one moment almost vomiting sexual disgust, the next caressing Claudio in a manner that suggests the nunnery is her refuge from an incestuous passion',[14] was left alone at the end, circling the stage, 'plainly in an agony of doubt'.[15] But by far the most extreme reaction was Penelope Wilton's as Isabella in Jonathan Miller's production the same year. There was no sex or gentleness in this Isabella, played as 'a flat chested, flat footed nun in black rubber soled shoes, clutching with purple hands a nasty handbag, into which she claws for a handkerchief to scarify her raw nose'.[16]. Her rejection of the Duke was absolute, and there was no question of her intention to return forever to the convent from which Lucio had reluctantly coaxed her in I.iv. For this Isabella, 'More than our brother is our chastity' was unquestionably the key to her character, and we can well imagine the fury with which she attacked Claudio in III.i for so much as suggesting she might still save him.[17]

Still more complex is the character of Hamlet, unquestionably the most difficult character in all Shakespearean drama to grasp. Any number of subtexts are available to the actor playing this role, though he probably will have to alter the subtext as he perceives the character of Hamlet itself altering. At the outset, Hamlet is alienated, grief-stricken, totally alone in the court of King Claudius, the man who has married his mother within a month of his father's death. Hostile and unhappy, he sounds the keynote to his disposition in his opening lines, 'A little more than kin and less than kind'; 'I am too much in the sun'; 'I know not seems'. His subtext may be inferred from the last lines of his first soliloquy: 'It is not, nor it cannot come to good, / But break my heart, for I must hold my tongue' (I.ii.158-159). Thus Gordon Craig conceived Hamlet for his famous Moscow Art Theatre production of 1912, in which Vasili Ivanovich Kachalov played the prince: 'All the tragedy of Hamlet is his isolation. And the background of this isolation is the court, a world of pretence. . . .'[18] Hamlet, like his father, is the best of men, the only good man in an evil environment which it becomes his duty, after hearing the Ghost's story, to purge of wickedness ('The time is out of joint – O cursed spite, / That ever I was born to set it right', I.v.188-189).

Hamlet's reluctance to take immediate action has been many times examined, and many explanations for his delay have been offered. Perhaps the most notorious explanation is the one offered by Freud's disciple, Ernest Jones. As Francis Fergusson has explained, the Oedipus complex Jones saw as the main force underlying Hamlet's inaction is definitely in the play. Shakespeare did not require Freud's theorizing to observe the phenomenon upon which the theory was based, or rather to sense and feel deeply the kind of problem a young, sensitive young man in Hamlet's position confronts. When during the play-within-the-play, 'The Murder of Gonzago', Hamlet identifies Lucianus as 'nephew to the king' (III.ii.244), he identifies himself indirectly but still very closely with the murderer of the Player King, his father's surrogate.[19] This is proof positive that Oedipal feelings are at work. But as Fergusson shows, they are only a small part of what Hamlet feels and what the play presents; they do not govern the entire structure of the tragedy, which is involved as well with moral issues of murder and usurpation, vengeance, and loyalty, to say nothing of other emotional or psychological involvements, such as Hamlet's with Ophelia or with his schoolfellows, Rosencrantz, Guildenstern, and especially Horatio.

Overemphasis on Freudian interpretation was what most of all marred Laurence Olivier's film version of the play. As Guthrie remarks, the motto for the film, 'This is the story of a young man who could not make up his mind', was not only a gross simplification, it was in actual fact contradicted at nearly every point by Olivier's portrayal of the Prince. How could Hamlet be irresolute or incapable of action in view of the determined and efficient way in which he was seen to carry through the intrigue with the Players, the ruthless break with Ophelia, the forcible interview with his mother, the stabbing (albeit mistaken as to the victim's identity) of Polonius, the hoisting of Rosencrantz and Guildenstern with their own petard, the grapple with the pirates, the struggle with Laertes in Ophelia's grave?[20] So much for the man who could not make up his mind. But the film also erred in focusing insistently on Hamlet's attitude toward his mother, wrestling with her on a bed in the Closet Scene, for example, where no bed belongs (this is the Queen's dressing chamber, not her bedroom). In the final shots of the film, as Hamlet's body is being carried to the ramparts, the camera pauses before this bed in a manner that is both reminiscent and highly suggestive. Thus Olivier chose two subtexts for his interpretation of Hamlet, one not so much wrong as exaggerated, the other belied by his own vigorous rendition of the role.

In choosing a subtext, therefore, the actor must be extremely careful not to choose one that might lead to oversimplifying or exaggerating the complex nature of the character, whether in tragedy, comedy, or history play. Shakespeare's major characters tend in every genre[21] to be highly complex individuals, motivated by conflicting ideas and attitudes that reductive interpretation falsifies, whether in dramatic representation or in critical analysis. The actor's search for subtext will help penetrate to the character's inner core, the deeper psychological truth, as Stanislavski argued. At the same time the actor – and the audience – must realize that a subtext does not define the character completely. Interactions with other characters are also of utmost importance, the perspective an actor gains when, as Stanislavski says, he or she finds 'the calculated, harmonious inter-relationship and distribution of the parts in a whole play or role'.[22] The test of a truly useful subtext, finally, may well be its resistance to easy formulation in a phrase or quotation, unless that phrase or quote is itself richly ambiguous or complex.

CHAPTER V

Finding the language

Elizabethan enthusiasm for language – words, rhetoric, logic, argument – is well known, though perhaps not well understood, much less shared, in our day. Shakespeare fully participated in his contemporaries' exuberance and surpassed them in coining new words, refashioning old ones, above all providing structures that capitalized on the zest for language. While it would be a mistake to think that even in his most linguistically ebullient plays, such as *Love's Labour's Lost*, he was solely or chiefly interested in words for their own sake, it is true that he took great interest and pleasure in language. Therein lies a major problem for us. Reading as we run – if we read (more often we are listening, but to music rather than words) – we quickly tire of the apparent convolutions of older verse or prose. Don Marquis sounded a familiar note when Archy heard the demand for a good rousing plot, and not too much damned poetry!

How can modern audiences deal with this problem of Shakespeare's language? In *Playing Shakespeare* John Barton confronts the problem head on in his discussion of the 'two traditions'. On the one hand, there is Shakespeare's text, with all its rich verbal texture; on the other is the modern drama, with its short, sometimes curt dialogue.[1] Earlier, Richard David expressed it this way:

> Dialogue, as such, was less essential to Elizabethan drama than it is to most modern plays. There were, of course, the flytings

and contests of wit; there were also, in the early plays, those decorative patterns of which the stichomuthia [sic] of Richard and Elizabeth, or the alternating dirge over Juliet, are obvious examples. . . . These passages are, however, static in their effect; that is, they may define various emotions in the speaker and arouse them in the audience, but they cause no spiritual development or revolution in either. The true dramatic crises, the dynamic effects which do achieve this, are found in single speeches. For, the feelings of an Elizabethan drama being always explicit, always elaborated in the text, it was possible to sum up fully and clearly, in the reaction of a single character, a situation and its emotional consequences which to-day would have to be deduced from the interaction of half a dozen speeches.[2]

The Elizabethans were following the tradition of classical drama, after all, and were heavily influenced by it as well as by more recent Renaissance drama and rhetoric. These traditions have long been lost for most modern audiences. John Barton, however, describes a number of ways actors can overcome the disadvantages time has brought, ways through which they can wed the 'two traditions', the old and the new. He emphasizes the need to use the verse, to let it help the actor, who on his part must make the words his own, must make them sound spontaneous, fresh, newly minted. Avoiding a general emotional overlay, the actor must zero in on the specifics, take the audience with him, and enter fully into the dynamics inherent in the language.

Barton's concern in his book, as in the television tapes it transcribes, is to help actors cope with and master the difficulties of Shakespeare's speeches. He warns directors not to discuss 'poetry' with actors at first, or risk frightening them into near paralysis. Instead, he refers to 'heightened language', which appears both in verse and prose. Essential in either case is grasping the proper stresses and rhythms, using the verse or in prose using the phrasing Shakespeare offers. As Barton says, it is altogether too easy, for both actor and audience, to settle for the general gist of a speech and the emotional overlay, rather than attend to the specific words and the meanings they are used to convey.

In the actual illustrations, Barton's book is less useful than his television tapes. These present actors from the Royal Shakespeare Company reading Shakespeare's lines in various ways, sometimes exaggerating one approach or another to point up the various pitfalls an actor is liable to stumble into, then showing how – by paying careful attention to the words – the actor can deliver the lines much more effectively. While Barton is coaching the actors, he is also coaching the audience, most immediately his television audience, and through them the theatregoing audience. For the audience, too, must find the language in Shakespeare's plays, grasp it, and enjoy it. How is this done?

I shall begin with something that may sound very heretical and even contradictory, considering the earlier emphasis on finding the text. For the theatregoer, it is not essential to have read the play in advance of the performance. Certainly, it will help to do so. The more familiarity we have with the text, the better prepared we are to comprehend, to analyse and evaluate, the production of a Shakespeare play. But if the production is competent, if the actors are well trained in language as well as the other aspects of performance, we can derive from it a good deal of pleasure and satisfaction – as well as comprehension – without knowing the text intimately or even at all. What is essential is that we remain attentive and alert and work with the actors to bring Shakespeare's play alive in our consciousness.

Consciousness. That is the key. And imagination. Listen to Shakespeare's Chorus at the opening of *Henry V*, lines that merit repeated study:

> O for a Muse of fire, that would ascend
> The brightest heaven of invention!
> A kingdom for a stage, princes to act,
> And monarchs to behold the swelling scene!
> Then should the warlike Harry, like himself,
> Assume the port of Mars, and at his heels
> (Leash'd in, like hounds) should famine, sword, and fire
> Crouch for employment. But pardon, gentles all,
> The flat unraised spirits that hath dar'd
> On this unworthy scaffold to bring forth
> So great an object. Can this cockpit hold
> The vasty fields of France? Or may we cram
> Within this wooden O the very casques
> That did affright the air at Agincourt?
> O, pardon! since a crooked figure may
> Attest in little place a million,
> And let us, ciphers to this great accompt,
> On your imaginary forces work.
> Suppose within the girdle of these walls
> Are now confin'd two mighty monarchies,
> Whose high, upreared, and abutting fronts
> The perilous narrow ocean parts asunder.
> Piece out our imperfections with your thoughts;
> Into a thousand parts divide one man,

And make imaginary puissance;
Think, when we talk of horses, that you see them
. Printing their proud hoofs i' th' receiving earth;
For 'tis your thoughts that now must deck our kings,
Carry them here and there, jumping o'er times,
Turning th' accomplishment of many years
Into an hour-glass: for the which supply,
Admit me Chorus to this history;
Who, Prologue-like, your humble patience pray,
Gently to hear, kindly to judge, our play.

As in any long verse speech – and there are many in Shakespeare's plays – the phrasing suggested by the rhythm, caesuras, and logic dictate how the speech must be divided into segments and accordingly modulated.[3] In this speech, the Chorus has clear designs upon the audience, but he must hook their attention from the start – and keep it hooked – or he will not realize his purpose, which is to urge the audience to become an active participant in the drama that is about to unfold. The fieriest Muse in heaven will avail exactly nothing if the Chorus fails to engage the audience, that is, get them to 'work' their imaginary forces. Shakespeare has given a lot of help, but only the actor playing the Chorus can bring it off. How?

He must, first of all, carefully modulate the important words that follow after the first four exclamatory lines. As he speaks, 'famine, sword, and fire' must become leashed hounds indeed, not merely allegorical abstractions. Then, seeing himself all but carried away, he must take the audience with him in his apology, win their sympathy as he acknowledges the limitations on the art of drama, but above all gain their willing cooperation so that by line 19 their imaginations are already at work, 'piecing out' the 'imperfections' of dramatic representation. He can only accomplish this, as Barton says, by making the words his words, not something on a printed script, but seemingly uttered for the first time.[4] He must carry the conviction that what he says is not only plausible, but true: the audience can and will do what he asks them; he believes this, so they do.

What happens in the audience, then? Do they not discover their own 'imaginary puissance'? As the Chorus imagines vast armies and horses' proud hoofs 'printing' the earth, won't the audience 'see' them, too, that is, if they are willing to work to this end and are using their visual imagination? Later in Act IV, as the armies gather at Agincourt, if the Chorus has made the words his own – as Barton instructs David Suchet to do – he will help the audience see and feel and hear the activity of the opposing camps.[5] In this highly episodic play, the job of the Chorus is not just to keep things moving, but to keep the audience imaginatively active, preventing a lapse into the easy passivity of being merely entertained. They must 'work'. But if the Chorus is not working hard to make this happen, it won't.

Modulation, phrasing, pauses – all these aspects of careful and precise articulation help the audience find the language they need to engage their imagination. Stresses at the right places, pitch, volume, and tone of voice, and above all pacing are also essential means that the actor has to keep the audience alert and active; making Shakespeare's words his own helps them become the audience's, too. And when they become ours, we can follow what is happening, join in the action, 'empathize' to the extent necessary to become sufficiently involved. It then becomes no difficult thing to turn the accomplishment of many years into an hour-glass, or to deck the kings of England and of France and carry them back and forth over land or sea. The autonomy of the imagination is thereby not only confirmed, it is exercised, stretched, triumphant.

Finding the language thus becomes crucial for actor and audience alike if they are to experience fully what happens in a Shakespeare play. As Harley Granville-Barker long ago said, the speaking of the verse is the foundation of all study when it comes to staging the plays.[6] The 'poetry' of it need not, and should not, become an inhibiting influence; on the contrary, when rightly appreciated and understood, it becomes the ultimate source of Shakespeare's power. At its best, conciseness, richness, irony are among the many attributes that help keep his language alive and vital, and as we respond to those elements of language, we become alive and vital with it. In *Players of Shakespeare*, Michael Pennington describes how John Barton encouraged him to use the language as 'a *necessary* funnel for the emotions' when playing Hamlet:

> This may sound obvious, but in a part as emotionally turbulent as Hamlet the actor may sometimes allow a tide of feeling to distort highly-wrought areas of language and so make them obscure. In fact of course the feelings require those words, and only those words, to define them and make them communicable – it is all one thing, the feeling, the pressure, the need to speak, the image that defines. It can be like pressing a tornado through the eye of a needle, but a persistent attention to colour, texture, rhythm and characteristic music goes beyond textual piety to become an emotional necessity.[7]

In the theatre we may not grasp Shakespeare's every image, every nuance, but is it absolutely essential that we should? Is it not possible, if we keep alert and 'work', nevertheless to get a great deal? The more we work, the more we grasp; our response will be fuller, and our experience of the play also will be more completely satisfying.[8] Tony Church demonstrates how in *Henry V*, I.ii, the Archbishop of Canterbury's extremely long and difficult speech interpreting Salic law can be made comprehensible – and occasionally deliberately funny – if properly rendered. His actual delivery of course cannot be captured in the book, *Playing Shakespeare*, but Barton's comments to him are highly instructive:

> It's a solemn situation with the council all around, and yet the speech is in part comic. So, go first for the tortuous argument and see if you can make us follow it clearly. But keep a balance. You must keep two balls in the air, political seriousness and character comedy. . . . there are two other points to remember. First, you'll need variety, because monotony or sticking to one tempo in a long speech is fatal. And, secondly, you mustn't be too quick or too slow but you must think quickly. If you do, you'll find the natural tempo. (pp. 92-93).

If this speech, with all its rhetorical and legal complications, can be made intelligible, cannot the most 'poetical' speeches be made comprehensible as well? Then what is understood may be enjoyed, both as poetry and as dramatic dialogue.

Take, for example, one of King Lear's great speeches in the storm scenes. Fleeing from the tyranny of his older daughters, Lear is nearly driven mad, but his wits have not quite turned – not yet. Standing outside Poor Tom's hovel, he is entreated by Kent to enter, but Lear tells him and then his Fool to enter first – untypically putting others before himself – and then speaks briefly in an important soliloquy:

> *Kent.* Good my lord, enter here.
> *Lear.* Prithee go in thyself, seek thine own ease.
> This tempest will not give me leave to ponder
> On things would hurt me more. But I'll go in.
> [*To the Fool*] In, boy, go first. – You houseless poverty –
> Nay, get thee in; I'll pray, and then I'll sleep.
>   *Exit* [*Fool*].
> Poor naked wretches, whereso'er you are,
> That bide the pelting of this pitiless storm,
> How shall your houseless heads and unfed sides,
> Your [loop'd] and window'd raggedness, defend you

From seasons such as these? O, I have ta'en
Too little care of this! Take physic, pomp,
Expose thyself to feel what wretches feel,
That thou mayst shake the superflux to them
And show the heavens more just. (III.iv.22-36)

However reluctantly, Kent and the Fool enter the hovel first, leaving Lear alone to ponder things that would hurt him more than the raging tempest, but not what would hurt him most – his daughters' cruel ingratitude. He has begun to think deeply and sensitively about persons other than himself, as signalled earlier by 'I did her wrong' (I.v.24) and here by his consideration for Kent and the Fool. He then carries his thought forward to a general concern for the 'Poor naked wretches' abroad in his kingdom. The generalized concern, however, quickly becomes specific and detailed, sounded first by the insistent drumbeat of the weather ('That *b*ide the *p*elting of this *p*itiless storm'), then through the images of 'houseless heads and unfed sides' and the metaphors of 'loop'd and window'd raggedness'. Using our visual imagination, we the working audience see the torn rags that barely hide the starving wretches and feel, with Lear, compassion for their plight. The startling recognition – 'O, I have ta'en / Too little care of this!' – brings a sharp pang of guilt, which Lear initially expresses in a deep sigh. Then comes the difficult moral: put yourself in their places, you who live in luxury ('pomp'), so that you may be moved to surrender the excess you do not need ('the superflux'), and by giving it to the poor demonstrate how heaven can be more just than we realize.

On the page, the speech may appear somewhat contorted, the words strange and therefore difficult; but the actor, following Shakespeare's signals within the verse, and grasping the specific as well as the general significance of the words, can make the lines immediately and fully intelligible. More than intelligible, by making the speech his own, he brings the words directly home to the audience so that we participate with him in both the feeling and the meaning of the lines. With him, we experience both Lear's physical and mental storm and recognize with distress the social injustice that leaves the poor unprotected to the elements. We empathize, or identify, with Lear at this moment – we feel both his guilt and his pain – in precisely the way Shakespeare means us to do, having found the language and, through the language, the essential qualities of the dramatic moment.

The actress playing Desdemona in *Othello* faces a different kind of challenge in her speech about 'poor Barbary'. The lines are far from contorted; their rhythms are almost those of prose, helped by irregular stresses, relatively simple diction and syntax, and the forward movement of sense that extends to run-on lines. Where then does the challenge lie? Is it in avoiding oversentimentalizing a very poignant expression of nostalgia and a presentiment of doom?

> My mother had a maid call'd Barbary;
> She was in love, and he she lov'd prov'd mad,
> And did forsake her. She had a song of 'Willow',
> An old thing 'twas, but it express'd her fortune,
> And she died singing it. That song tonight
> Will not go from my mind; I have much ado
> But to go hang my head all at one side
> And sing it like poor Barbary. (IV.iii.26-33)

If the actress finds the right tone and tempo for this speech, she can also avoid sounding maudlin in the Willow Song, when it comes a few lines later. A touch of self-deprecating humour at lines 30-33 will not be amiss, if delivered with a delicacy and gentleness consistent with the rest of the speech, which is above all delicate and gentle and not overly emotional.[9] The problem here is not comprehension but a more subtle one of sensibility; during the scene the actress and the audience must keep precisely in tune with each other and with Shakespeare's words.

Careful articulation, sensitively modulated speaking, newly minting the words – these are some of the ways the actor can help audiences find the language of Shakespeare's plays, help us, that is, to become active and responsive, and – by using our visual imagination as well as our sensibilities – to co-operate in the experience of performance. But this is not all. Audiences need to recognize that Shakespeare's dramatic language is also highly complex; other aspects of it demand careful attention, too, if they are to be properly mastered. Irony and ambiguity and words that have a resonance beyond their denotative sense require an attentive ear. For example, as many critics have noticed, *nothing* recurs throughout the first three acts of *King Lear*, from the opening dialogue between the old king and Cordelia, to the Fool's riddling speeches, to Lear's climactic 'I will be the pattern of all patience, I will say nothing' (III.ii.37). The actors must release the heavy charge of energy in the word with neither crude nor obvious mouthings. The slightest pause before Lear's 'nothing' at III.ii.37 should be sufficient to make the necessary connections, if the audience is alert to what is happening.

Shakespeare and his audiences, it is well known, loved wordplay of all kinds. Much of it is still funny today, though the point of some of it is doubtless irrecoverably lost on a modern audience and needs to be cut. (What is sadder than to see an actor trying to force a laugh, and getting it only from the actors he or she is playing to?) Only the scholar, learned in philology, will pick up the pun in Touchstone's line, 'Ay, now I am in Arden, the more fool I' (*As You Like It*, II.iv.16). The line is intelligible enough without the pun and can be retained, but how many will catch Touchstone's pun on *harden*, the coarse smock he is apparently wearing over his motley coat?[10] The opening dialogue between Capulet's servants, Sampson and Gregory, contains a great many puns and other quibbles which can be funny enough if played with sufficient verve, giving the audience appropriate clues by intonation, facial expressions, and gestures so that even the more obscure jokes can be grasped. Sometimes, if a pun is practically spelled out for us, we can get it readily enough, as Kathleen Widdoes playing Beatrice pronounces 'Signior Mountanto' ('Signior Mount-on-to'). But that is really pushing the joke, and a performance can tolerate only a little of this sort of thing.

Ambiguities can be serious as well as funny – sometimes both at the same time. Mercutio comments on the wound Tybalt has given him: '. . . 'tis not so deep as a well, nor so wide as a church-door, but 'tis enough, 'twill serve. Ask for me to-morrow, and you shall find me a grave man' (*Romeo and Juliet*, III.ii.96-98). Here he puns on *grave* = 'serious' + 'in my grave', an appropriate valedictory utterance by one whose speeches typically were both serious and joking. Hamlet's first line, 'A little more than kin and less than kind' (I.ii.65), contains multiple puns on *kin* and *kind*, and again this is an appropriate utterance for someone who will confront throughout the play the ironies and ambiguities of his experience, often in wild and whirling words. His next line emphasizes this attitude with further punning on *sun-son* in the dialogue with Claudius:

> *Claudius.* How is it that the clouds still hang on you?
> *Hamlet.* Not so, my lord, I am too much in the sun. (I.ii.66-67)

Claudius is of course speaking metaphorically, referring to Hamlet's mourning clothes as well as his disposition and comportment, when Hamlet takes him up and under the protection of ambiguity delivers a shrewd reply, playing on ambiguities that concern his becoming Claudius's stepson, Claudius's usurpation of the throne, and the present necessity to appear and speak in public.[11]

The use of ambiguity thus permits Shakespeare's characters to say several things at once. It is as close as a human being can ever get to singing in chords, so to speak, as when Macbeth invokes 'seeling' night to 'Cancel and tear to pieces that great bond' which keeps him 'pale' (III.i.46-50), or earlier when Lady Macbeth says that she will 'gild the faces of the grooms withal', so that Duncan's murder must seem their 'guilt' (II.ii.53-54).[12] In the complex world of human thought and action it is of the utmost importance that language of this kind is employed and understood. No one denies that it is difficult, especially when it is used in a long and unfamiliar speech that involves other difficulties of comprehension already discussed. The audience must stay alert and be prepared for words that will carry more than one meaning, often several meanings, even contradictory ones. We are all familiar with Mark Antony's funeral oration and his use of irony, a particular form of ambiguity. At first, he appears sincere in referring to Brutus, Cassius, and the others as 'honorable men', but as the speech unfolds it becomes clear through frequent repetitions and different contexts that he means the opposite. Falstaff's language is rich in ambiguities of all kinds; it is an essential part of his wit and reveals a keen awareness of what is happening around him. In the attack upon the travellers at Gad's Hill, however, he surprises us with a new kind of irony, as he cries out:

> Hang ye, gorbellied knaves, are ye undone? No, ye fat chuffs, I would your store were here! On, bacons, on! What, ye knaves, young men must live! You are grandjurors, are ye? We'll jure ye, faith. (*1 Henry IV*, II.ii.88-92)

Not only is kettle Falstaff calling the potbellied travellers black, he is also referring to himself and his confederates as 'young men' (compare line 85: 'they hate us youth'). We know that the white-haired knight is well on in years – that is part of his disgrace, that he should behave as he does in spite of his age. But in what sense is it also true that he is young and indeed the most youthful character in the play? If the audience is aware of these ironies and ambiguities, they will relish the scene in many ways, even if they are puzzled by the pun on *grandjurors-jure ye*, which they can ignore.[13]

Sometimes, Shakespeare's characters are endowed with what might be called unconscious ambiguities, that is, double or treble meanings of which they are, as characters, not themselves fully aware. This does not mean the audience should remain unaware of them – quite the reverse. The most obvious form of unwitting ambiguity is, of course, the malapropism, or the misuse of language by a character for comic and sometimes other effect, as in Elbow's complaint against Pompey and Froth in *Measure for Measure*:

> *Elbow.* If it please your honor, I am the poor Duke's constable, and my name is Elbow. I do lean upon justice, sir, and do bring in here before your good honor two notorious benefactors.
> *Angelo.* Benefactors? Well; what benefactors are they? Are they not malefactors?
> *Elbow.* If it please your honor, I know not well what they are; but precise villains they are, that I am sure of, and void of all profanation in the world that good Christians ought to have.
> (II.i.46-56)

That Shakespeare expects us to pick up unintended ambiguities is clear from the opening scene of *Henry IV, Part One*. King Henry has been telling his lords about brave Hotspur's exploits in Scotland, when Westmoreland comments, 'In faith, / It is a conquest for a prince to boast of' (I.i.75-76). Without meaning to, Westmoreland has struck a sensitive nerve in Henry, who takes *prince* literally and associates the remark with his son (the Prince of Wales), who has been behaving quite differently with his cronies in Eastcheap. Similarly, M. M. Mahood regards the opening lines of *Romeo and Juliet* as 'a kind of verbal tuning up which quickens our ear for the great music to come'. The bawdry, funny in itself, also has a dramatic function 'to make explicit, at the beginning of this love tragedy, one possible relationship between man and woman: a brutal male dominance expressed in sadistic quibbles'.[14] Suggestions of other kinds of relationship soon follow with Romeo's entrance, and the play as a whole explores a wide range of attitudes and ideas about love.

Ambiguities often involve images, and patterns of images and ambiguities in Shakespeare's plays, once discerned, help an audience grasp the play's underlying thematic structure and other aspects of its dramaturgy. In what is by now a classic essay of its kind, 'The Naked Babe and the Cloak of Manliness', Cleanth Brooks has shown how Shakespeare's imagery in *Macbeth* becomes the vehicle for some its most powerful symbolism.[15] Disease imagery in *Hamlet*, crucifixion imagery in *Richard II*, light imagery in *Romeo and Juliet* are other significant patterns that, when grasped, make the experience of the plays richer and deeper for an audience attuned to Shakespeare's language.[16] That Shakespeare thought in images appears an indisputable fact, and appreciating the imagery not as mere decoration but as an integral and functioning part of his dramatic language is an essential part of the intelligent theatregoer's equipment. Like other Elizabethans, Shakespeare was especially fond of the imagery of conception and exploited both its literal and figurative senses, often playing one off against the other with sometimes ironic effect. In *Measure for Measure*, for example, Angelo meditates on his attempted seduction of Isabella and uses a series of images through which, ironically, he sees himself becoming impregnated with evil. 'She speaks, and 'tis / Such sense that my sense breeds with it' (II.ii.141-142), he says in an aside during their first meeting. Just before their second encounter he contemplates 'the strong and swelling evil' of his 'conception' (II.iv.6)7); and when he thinks he has carried out the seduction, he comments to himself: 'This deed unshapes me quite, makes me unpregnant / And dull to all proceedings' (IV.iv.20-21). The attentive audience, visualizing the imagery, grasps at once the multiple, underlying ironies that at the end of the play will be fully revealed and largely, if not entirely, resolved.

Shakespeare's language and particularly his imagery may be so suggestive that a director or set designer will sometimes take a cue from it and design a production around a dominant or significant motif. Thus in John Barton's *Hamlet* (1981) the stage metaphors used throughout the play (e.g., 'They are actions that a man may play', I.ii.84) apparently suggested the setting of a stage-like platform upon which the actors performed and around or behind which were left various props, such as a suit of armour (which provided a convenient hiding place for Polonius's eavesdropping). The frequent references to blood in *Macbeth* have led many designers to bathe the stage in red light throughout the central scenes, although in his film Orson Welles took a different cue. From the invocations to darkness and night uttered by both Macbeth and his wife, Welles unnaturally darkened the Scottish landscape – until IV.iii, when the scene shifts to Edward the Confessor's England, and sunlight at last bursts forth.

CHAPTER VI

Finding the stage business, music, and other effects

When in *King John*, III.i, Kings Philip of France and John of England enter at line 74, they are in a jovial mood, having just effected a happy end to their armed conflict in Act II. Throughout most of the scene, they hold hands, a sign of their newly won amity, although precisely when or where the handshake occurs the text does not indicate. When Cardinal Pandulph, the Pope's legate, enters, he accuses John of insubordination and demands that he submit to the papal see or suffer the consequences of excommunication. He is equally severe to Philip. If John does not submit, Philip must break from him or risk similar treatment:

> Philip of France, on peril of a curse,
> Let go the hand of that arch-heretic,
> And raise the power of France upon his head,
> Unless he do submit himself to Rome. (III.i.191-194)

For over a hundred lines the handshake remains a central focus in the debate and in Philip's dilemma: if Philip retains his friendship with John, he will bring down the Church's wrath upon himself and his kingdom; if he renounces the 'deep-sworn faith, peace, amity, true love' (l. 231) so recently concluded between John and himself, war will resume, with heavy bloodshed on both sides. He clings to John's hand, implores Pandulph to find some alternative to either disaster, but all in vain. Pandulph is adamant; so is John. Finally, at line 320, Philip acquiesces to the Church, and with the words 'England, I will fall from thee', drops John's hand.[1]

The scene is a good example of how Shakespeare intended stage business, or visual imagery (for that is what it often is), to complement or extend the significance of dialogue. As Ann Pasternak Slater has shown in *Shakespeare the Director*, the plays are full of clues to how a scene is or should be played. But the stage directions are frequently incomplete or lacking altogether, and sometimes we cannot readily determine whether they are Shakespeare's or others' – perhaps actors' – interpolations. The bracketed stage directions of responsible modern editions show where editors have emended to help clarify the situation for the reader or actor, though earlier editors did not always indicate where there were additions to or emendations of the text. This is not a serious problem when it involves adding an obviously missing 'Exit' or 'Exeunt', but it can become one if the text does not make clear whether characters are present or not, or what gestures or actions they should perform when they have no lines.[2]

At the other extreme, we find directors adding much uncalled-for stage business, sometimes to enliven a scene, sometimes to heighten the comedy or tragedy, sometimes just to show off their inventiveness. The Royal Shakespeare Company's production of *The Taming of the Shrew* in 1978, directed by Michael Bogdanov, began with a great deal of stage business – not all of it on the stage! As the audience entered the theatre and took their seats, it became increasingly evident that one of the ushers was having difficulty seating a man who became more and more boisterous and disruptive. Finally, he jumped up on the stage where the scenery for the Induction was in place (the RSC, like other companies, has long since eschewed curtains) and promptly began tearing the set apart. Not until others emerged from the wings and he was subdued with a sedative did the audience realize that the man was the actor Jonathan Pryce playing Christopher Sly. On some evenings, it has been said, members of the audience became so alarmed that they called the police before they realized what was happening.

Well, that is one way to start a play and get the audience's attention. Not, perhaps, the best way, though it was effective for a modern-dress production that emphasized the violence inherent in the script. Without question, the director there took a great deal of licence, and was accordingly criticized. John Barton's RSC production of *Hamlet* a few years later (1981) did not go quite so far when, in the Closet Scene (III.iv), he had Gertrude actually see the Ghost and faint. In a more recent production of the play in Stratford, Ontario (1986), in the same scene or just afterwards, as Hamlet is 'lugging the guts [of Polonius] into the neighbor room', Ophelia enters and sees him, and this becomes the trigger for her madness.

If none of the stage business just described is called for by the script, by what warrant has it been introduced? How much license can a director take? What is the purpose and justification for added business of this kind? When does it succeed, and on what basis, and when does it fail? These are some of the questions the theatregoer may well ask when viewing a performance of Shakespeare's plays, but it may not always be easy to find a clear or convincing answer.

The essential question, of course, is how does the added business or other stage effect illuminate something in the play that is really there but might otherwise be obscure or entirely hidden away. To have Ophelia see Hamlet carry her father's corpse unceremoniously away is a *coup de théâtre* on the same order as having Lear kill his Fool in the mad trial scene (III.vi), as Adrian Noble directed Michael Gambon to do. They clarify aspects of the text, though in so doing they may make too vivid and explicit what Shakespeare meant to remain suggestive or ambiguous. Undoubtedly, a primary cause of Ophelia's madness – though not the only one – is the fact that her lover has slain her father. But less extreme alternatives are available to show Ophelia's impending breakdown, as the actress playing Ophelia to Vittorio Gassman's Hamlet in Rome (1952) demonstrated. At the end of the Nunnery Scene, she delivered the lines that begin 'O, what a noble mind is here o'erthrown!' (III.i.150) with such emotion that one sensed her own mind going.

The situation in *King Lear* is more complicated. Lear's cryptic line, 'And my poor fool is hang'd!' (V.iii.306), has never been satisfactorily explained and remains ambiguous. It could refer to Cordelia, who has been hanged (Lear boasts of killing 'the slave that was a-hanging thee', l. 275), in which case *fool* in line 306 is a term of endearment for his dead daughter. But it could also refer to the Fool, whose disappearance after III.vi remains a mystery. If one kills the thing he loves, as Noble's interpretation seems to indicate, then Lear's killing his Fool, however unintentionally but nonetheless directly, makes a certain kind of sense. On the other hand, in Grigori Kozintsev's film version of the play, the Fool does not die. At the end, as the bodies of Lear, Cordelia, and the others are being carried off, he is seen sitting playing his flute, until one of the litter bearers, finding the Fool in the way, gives him a kick. A different kind of stage business, perhaps, but in its way powerfully effective, too.

The liberty of invention may sometimes find dimensions to a scene or episode that may not have been intended by Shakespeare but that, once discovered, deepen our understanding of what is happening. In the Royal Shakespeare Company's production of *As You Like It* in 1985, the imaginative director (Adrian Noble again) was guilty of much gimmickry and irrelevant busyness, but he was also responsible for some excellent touches – and more than touches – that extended the action of the play without disrupting it. The hunting episode (IV.ii), for example, was played as if it were Celia's dream, since Celia concludes IV.i with the line, 'And I'll sleep' and (in this production) lies down. Roger Warren describes what followed: 'Jaques drew a bloodstained sheet across [Celia] as she slept, and the lords then pursued her around the stage as if she were the hunted deer. She had obviously had an erotic dream, a sexual awakening, and was therefore especially receptive to Oliver on his arrival, a point reinforced by the little laugh of sexual shock at his reference to the snake from which Orlando had saved him.'[3] Did Shakespeare have anything like this in mind when he wrote Act IV? Does it matter whether he did or not? Or is the question really whether or not the stage business illuminates an aspect of the play that might otherwise remain hidden or obscured?

Consider another recent RSC production, *A Midsummer Night's Dream* (1986). The director, Bill Alexander, decided to double the roles of Hippolyta and Titania but not those of Theseus and Oberon. Here, he departed from the practice frequently followed since Peter Brook's landmark 1970 production, in which both Theseus and Hippolyta were doubled with their counterparts in the forest. Why did Alexander go only half way? Why did he also add a scene between I.i and ii where Hippolyta paces outside the court and encounters, wordlessly, Bottom as he hurries to meet Peter Quince and the others to begin rehearsals? And at the end of the play, as the fairies led by Oberon enter unseen by the court (who are still on stage), why does Hippolyta move over and take her place among them, once again as Titania although still in the costume of Hippolyta? Are the central acts of the play after all only Hippolyta's dream, as Alexander conceives the action? Or is Hippolyta a creature of two worlds, capable of fulfilling her role of Theseus' duchess but not yet fully reconciled to it, as her brief appearance (as Hippolyta) in the forest in II.i further suggests?[4]

Directors may not only add stage business that is not called for in the text, they may sometimes alter or even delete business that is. In the second banquet scene, *Macbeth*, III.iv, for example, the Folio of 1623 gives the following stage direction at line 36: 'Enter the Ghost of Banquo, and sits in Macbeths place.' Macbeth apparently does not notice this until a few lines later, after Rosse has asked him to sit, and Macbeth replies: 'The table's full.' In the BBC television version of the play, however, no Ghost appears, and Macbeth (played by Nicol Williamson) quite clearly is hallucinating. So his wife, Lady Macbeth, believes, as she tries to calm him down and restore cheer to the feast:

> This is the very painting of your fear;
> This is the air-drawn dagger which you said
> Led you to Duncan. O, these flaws and starts
> (Imposters to true fear) would well become
> A woman's story at a winter's fire,
> Authoriz'd by her grandam. Shame itself,
> Why do you make such faces? When all's done,
> You look but on a stool. (60-67)

As the speech reminds us, Macbeth has hallucinated at least once before; is this another occasion? The original stage direction, which may or may not be Shakespeare's,[5] suggests that the Ghost is really there, though the others cannot see it. Does the director therefore have the option to remove it as a physical – or physical-seeming – presence on the stage? According to Marvin Rosenberg's researches, many have exercised precisely that option, often to good effect. Others have used substitute illusions to suggest the unreality of the Ghost, as Henry Irving did in 1875, also to good effect. 'The governing aesthetic consideration,' Rosenberg says, 'is that the image be as uncanny and frightening as possible within the limits of the tolerable. . . Would the imaginary terrify more than the "real"? What counts is what works in the theater.'[6]

Things don't always work well in the theater, no matter how ingenious or imaginative they may be. Richard David cites a number of examples of the director's or actor's inventiveness which misfired completely, spoiling or distorting the action of a scene. In the RSC production of *Henry IV, Part One* (1975), Hotspur (played by Stuart Wilson) developed an unwarranted jealousy of Prince Hal, to the point of falling into an epileptic fit at the mention of his name. This unjustified bit of business fortunately was dropped in later performances.[7] Although the overall reception of John Barton and Barry Kyle's production of *Troilus and Cressida* for the RSC in 1976 was highly favorable, it contained some notable blemishes, such as the way Pandarus (as played by David Waller) sang the song in III.i for Paris and Helen. The song is unquestionably obscene, but as David says, 'to have Pandarus mime its lubricities with a giant bolster is (somewhat to misapply the metaphor) gilding the lily'.[8] To mention just one more example of misdirected stage business: In the otherwise powerful and effective production of *Macbeth* at The Other Place in Stratford-upon-Avon, 1976, the Sleepwalking Scene was marred, not by the presence of the Doctor, who should and must be there, but by his physical and vocal intrusiveness. Instead of remaining properly in the background as Lady Macbeth goes through her agony of guilt, he bent over his patient and, 'almost taking her pulse', destroyed both illusion and effect.[9]

Shakespeare's 'open silences', as Philip McGuire calls them, provide directors and actors with opportunities for inventiveness as well as interpretation. As we have noted (p. 46), Isabella's response to Duke Vincentio's proposal of marriage at the end of *Measure for Measure* is nowhere indicated in the text, either in the dialogue or in the stage directions. The actress playing the part must discover an appropriate reaction, for she can hardly remain both stationary and mute. At the end of *The Tempest*, as McGuire points out, there is a whole series of open silences involving Antonio, Miranda, and Ariel. How should Antonio respond to his brother Prospero's forgiveness? The text does not say (see V.i.126 ff.). The contrast with Sebastian's response suggests a sullen and dangerous acquiescence, but on the contrary Antonio could feel 'a penitence so intense and profound that no words can convey it', as in Robin Phillips' production at Stratford, Ontario (1976), where Antonio fell to his knees and Prospero, recognizing genuine repentance, took both his hands.[10]

The situation is different for Prospero's daughter, Miranda, who has no further lines after her expressive speech that ends with 'O brave new world / That has such people in it' (181-182). How does she act after that, while further revelations and reconciliations take place? Amazed and in awe, does she cling to Ferdinand, who has declared their betrothal, to his father Alonzo's gratification as well as his own? Or does she stand with Prospero, knowing that her time with him is now limited, after the years together on the magic island? Recent productions have explored these and other possibilities,[11] the stage business contributing to or clarifying the interpretation of the scene. Similarly, Ariel's reaction to his freedom raises some questions in which staging and the interpretation of character are closely related. Does he depart from Prospero with reluctance, after so many years of loyal service? Or does his silent exit indicate a renunciation of the bond that has kept him subservient ever since being released from the knotty pine in which Sycorax confined him? 'A *Tempest* that presents Ariel's silent departure after being granted freedom as a renunciation of Prospero,' McGuire says, 'differs significantly from one in which Ariel's silence suggests the mixture of joy and pain that Ariel himself feels as he and his master separate – Ariel moving into the freedom of the elements and Prospero rejoining the world of men.[12] Thus stage business is a major means by which actors and directors demonstrate their interpretation of the text, especially at places where Shakespeare himself offers little or no direction.[13] For the audience, the questions remain: Is the play intelligently and sensitively illuminated? Is something added that helps us understand the play's intention better, or are the additions intrusive and disruptive, moving the play off into another, irrelevant or distracting, direction?

These questions pertain as well to musical accompaniments and dance. Unquestionably, Shakespeare, like his contemporaries, loved music. If England under Elizabeth was not quite 'a nest of singing birds', yet there was much music written, played, and sung: the other arts flourished along with poetry and drama, but none more than music. The stage directions in Shakespeare's plays include many calls for music, not only for songs to be sung, but hautboys (= oboes), trumpets, lutes, etc., to be played. The distinction between a 'sennet' and a 'flourish' may have some significance, but the particular kinds of music used in a production are much more important. Similar concerns follow for dance and even more elaborate kinds of spectacle, such as the introduction of a masque in *The Tempest*.

Let us recognize at once that the music should be appropriate to the settings, costumes, and basic representation of the text. To retain Elizabethan music in a modern dress production is patently absurd. New music needs to be composed, like Hiroshi Sato's for Michael Bogdanov's RSC production of *Romeo and Juliet* in 1986.[14] A student production of *As You Like It* at the University of California, Davis, in 1968, did not alter settings and costumes, but clearly the intention was to bring the production up to date in as many other ways as possible. Duke Senior became a guru who first appears in the Forest of Arden sitting with his lords in a circle passing around a marijuana pipe! Thomas Morley's lovely music to the songs Shakespeare wrote might have fitted in here, but much better suited was the soft rock music, composed and sung by the students, who also accompanied themselves on guitars. Recall that this was California in 1968. It is doubtful whether such a production would be quite as suitable today.

A related but more difficult problem arose when Herbert Blau directed *King Lear* for the Actor's Workshop in the early 1960s. For Blau and his company at the time, King Lear seemed 'the most immediate' of Shakespeare's plays, the one that spoke most directly and insistently to those who had experienced deeply, or needed to experience deeply, everything that the post-Holocaust and post-Hiroshima age signified. As Blau has written in his essay on the production, 'To do the play in the twentieth century, confronted by the possibility of capricious extinction that we see in the death of Cordelia, is to realize how awfully "Thy life's a miracle".'[15] Although the historical setting for *King Lear* is Britain's distant, primordial past, Blau's company wanted to push further back, 'to drive backward, through time, behind forms, making our way through a disintegrated past to invent a culture of our own'.[16] The sets, costumes, and properties accordingly reflected that intention: everything was new-made for the production, even the swords forged by sculptor Robert Hudson. So was the music by composer Morton Subotnik, who provided an electronic score. Blau describes the unusual resources Subotnik found for his score and the way they were all put together for the storm scenes, which present the greatest technical problem in the play. Subotnick composed the sound by combining Lear's voice saying 'I' into an open piano; a single pure pitch; and a cello note (later used for the sleep music in IV.vii). However successful or not the effort was in actual performances (some members of the audience complained that the music drowned out Lear's speeches, but the acoustics in the theatre may have been partly responsible for that), the intention was right: to synchronize language, sound, and action so as to establish 'a perfect harmony of chaos, Lear and the storm locked by sound in a kind of cosmic embrace'.[17] Blau's emphasis that the storm should not be merely a background for the acting, but 'a steady presence', points further to an essential relation between sound and acting that productions of Shakespeare's plays ignore at their peril.

The synchrony of language, sound, and action was impossible to discover in the production of *A Midsummer Night's Dream* that London's Old Vic and the Sadlers' Wells Ballet brought to New York's old Metropolitan Opera House in the autumn of 1952. In a throwback to nineteenth-century production styles, heavy sets were imported – whole forests of trees – and very elaborate costumes. Mendelssohn's music was used throughout, but not as incidental music only: it became the music for ballet dances at frequent intervals in the show. For that is what the play became – a good show, one that could delight and entertain anyone who liked music and dance and spectacle and did not mind a bit of poetry, too. The corps de ballet was excellent, and Robert Helpmann's Oberon stands out a generation later as a marvelous combination of actor and dancer. Somewhere in the midst of all the splendour Shakespeare's play lurked, but it was not clear precisely where.

The Winter's Tale also invites innovations in music and dance, regardless of the setting, as in the Royal Shakespeare Company's production of 1986. As every director knows, the long fourth act presents a number of problems: after the intensities of Acts I-III, the action resumes in a relaxed, casual fashion, and includes scenes of merrymaking, song, and dance. The excellent comedian and actor, Joe Melia, took the part of Autolycus and introduced delightful music hall tunes, routines, and sound effects, such as birdcalls that sounded very much like 'cuckoos'. The music was new and appropriate to the setting and the action, and Melia won over the audience that had earlier been dazzled by spectacular effects in Act III, such as the enormous bear with electric blue eyes that rose up from a rear trap and devoured poor Antigonus, or Henry Goodman's winged Father Time that opened Act IV. Melia saw the challenge and met it in his own style and humour. Later in Act IV, composer Nigel Hess and choreographer Chrissy Wickham were less successful teaming up for a music and dance spectacular, 'Whither, O whither?' By far too jazzy for the setting and the action, the production number (the musical comedy term seems the best one here) failed to move the audience as it was meant to do and as Joe Melia had done. More to the point, it seemed an excrescence, something 'added to', not integrated or merged with everything else, as it should have been.

Music in films may serve other functions, but the audience who complains, 'Don't tell me how to feel!' is probably right: music can be obtrusive in just that way, overriding our direct response – or what would be our direct response – to language and action.[18] When the text has been disintegrated and then put back together in a radically different structure, music can provide bridges, or transitions, especially when changes in mood or atmosphere might otherwise seem too abrupt. Themes can be important, too, as in Olivier's or Kozinstev's films of *Hamlet*. Roger Manvell remarks on William Walton's score for Olivier's *Hamlet* and compares it with his score for *Henry V*, where music was used more sparingly, although it lent a 'rich colouring' to the atmosphere of the production. In *Hamlet*, the themes for the characters assume greater importance and are accordingly more fully developed.[19] By contrast, when Kozintsev and Dimitri Shostakovich collaborated again for the film of *King Lear*, Kozintsev rejected theme music for Cordelia (or anyone else) such as Shostakovich had written for Ophelia. Instead, he conceived of themes running through the whole tragedy, such as the 'call of death' or the Fool's playing on his pipe. In the editing, Kozintsev had to work hard to get the right blend of sound and image. He discovered the right fit almost by accident: starting with the first sequence with Cordelia that came to hand, he and E. A. Makhankova, the assistant editor with whom he had long worked, found a combination that blended music and image. In the process, the scene (which Kozintsev had watched many times) 'changed character. Something new and significant became apparent in our heroine. Shostakovich had written down Cordelia's inner light and the whole sequence was transformed.'[20]

What Shostakovich contributed was the work of a genius that could see beneath the surface reality and provide dimensions that are not added to the play but discovered from within it. Audiences may not be fully aware of what is happening, nor need they be. If the integration is complete and right, if it all comes together in the right way, the audience will respond to the full effect spontaneously and completely. And this is true not only of the music, but of the stage business and other effects as well.

[71]

CHAPTER VII

Finding coherence:
the overall interpretation

Up to now we have been concerned with the various parts of a production – finding the text, set design, characters, subtext, language, stage business, music, and other effects. It is therefore time to ask questions about overall interpretations or other ways in which productions find coherence. Although as human beings we are not compelled to live in a box called 'unity', as the critic R. P. Blackmur long ago warned, nevertheless we generally find unified works of art especially satisfying. We like things to hang together, to form a whole, to provide consistency and coherence. When they do not, we are troubled, find faults with a production, feel unsatisfied, cheated perhaps. Never mind that it may have been the deliberate intention of the author or director to leave us up in the air, unsatisfied by easy solutions or resolutions. Rightly or wrongly, we crave unity; we want coherence.

The absence of any recognizable coherence in the Royal Shakespeare's production of *Troilus and Cressida* at the Aldwych Theatre in 1981 was certainly a fault of that production. Sumptuous in each of its scenes – no expense was apparently spared to provide extraordinary spectacle, including elaborate costumes and settings – the production seemed loosely strung together (or not strung together at all) by the mere juxtaposition of episodes, episodes that appeared to have very little to do with one another.

As Roger Warren described the production in *Shakespeare Survey* 35 (1982): 'Terry Hands's *Troilus and Cressida* at the Aldwych represented the inconsistency of much of the current work of the RSC within a single production: strong performances and interesting interpretation alternated with excess and confusion' (p. 149). By contrast, Howard Davies's production in 1985 was all of a piece. While some theatregoers might not have enjoyed the interpretation of this difficult and ambiguous play – when it moved to the Barbican in 1986 it did not play to capacity audiences – they could see a very strong interpretation that held all parts of this anti-war, feminist version of the play together. The single set used for every scene (with only some minor shifting about of furniture) doubtless helped here, and the production grew in strength and purpose as it evolved over the course of two seasons. Its powerful coherence was all the more evident during early August 1986 when Juliet Stevenson, who played Cressida, became ill and an understudy temporarily took over her role. While Emma D'Inverno was competent, she lacked the vigor and forcefulness of Miss Stevenson and of the others in the cast. They had become a true ensemble, probably none of them replaceable by this time without evident loss – certainly not Cressida, upon whom much of the play depends even though her part is not large.

Ensemble acting is of course one good way to achieve coherence. When actors have been working together long and well, they pick up more than their cues from each other: they 'play off' one another in stimulating and exciting ways. Audiences may not be aware of this fact, nor need they be; it may only become apparent as in Davies's *Troilus and Cressida* when an understudy is required for a principal role. On the other hand, it is sometimes possible for an actor to change from a minor to a major role on very short notice, using a script in hand to read the lines, with so little awkwardness that it is hardly noticed by the audience. This happened at The Other Place in Stratford-upon-Avon in 1983, when Daniel Massey was suddenly called away to visit his dying father and could not play the lead in *The Time of Your Life*. Since no understudies are used for productions at The Other Place, an actor in a minor role took over Massey's part while someone else filled in for him, and the production continued. Because he had been in the play from the beginning and knew it and the others in the cast well, he could pick up the role and blend into the production easily and effectively.

That is one kind of coherence, the sort that comes from actors being well rehearsed together as a group, attuned to one another's subtleties of interpretation and delivery so that the production appears as a seamless garment. The director may rightly claim credit for some of this or all of it. But though the work does not end at opening night (he or she may still give the cast 'notes' afterwards from time to time), it is the actors' job to keep the production coherent, even as it continues to evolve from performance to performance. The director's responsibility, on the other hand, often begins before the cast is assembled, in thinking about the play and the way it should or could be staged most effectively and freshly.

Thus Peter Hall in his *Diaries* repeatedly refers to his ideas about a play long before any production has begun. For example, on February 18, 1975, he records his notion of how Marlowe's *Tamburlaine* might be staged, although he did not direct it until more than a year later:

> Hard work on *Tamburlaine*. I begin to understand it. I want to try it as a popular cartoon form of theatre, the actors discussing moral dilemmas directly with the audience. Each scene could have a strong emblem: a shepherd turning into a warrior; a scarlet banquet; three crowns carried onto the battlefield. All this to look like a stained glass window or picture book cartoon, and expressed in strong emotional rhetoric. More Italian than British. Get away from the wit, the cool and the intellect, to something more passionate and exposed.[1]

In an essay on 'Shakespeare and the Modern Director', Jonathan Miller records a similar way of proceeding:

> I've normally sketched out at least a theoretical construct of the production before I assemble the actors. I've already met with the designer and the costumer and developed an overall 'look' for the production. So with me there is a creative relationship with the actors that precedes any actual encounter simply by virtue of my having chosen one group of actors rather than another for various parts. I've already developed a rough idea of who it is that might have meant these lines or those, and that idea has informed my selection of this actor rather than that actor.[2]

Neither director is altogether bound by his initial conceptions. Miller goes on to say that his rehearsals tend to be 'more intuitive and haphazard and spontaneous' than one might expect from any explicit commitment to a theoretical position. A certain amount of freedom is necessary if one is to discover the latent ambiguities in the text or if actors are going to be allowed, let alone encouraged, to discover a useful subtext for the interpretations of their roles. The compromise occurs, as Miller expresses it, this way: 'Once I've decided what will be fundamental, I will emphasize that. But I also want to give the audience an experience of the complexities that accompany that primary emphasis' (p. 819).

The director decides what is 'fundamental', and working closely with a designer is crucial. The exigencies of modern productions require this early work before a cast is even assembled, because sets have to be built, costumes sewn, properties ordered, and so forth. All this takes time, much more time than the rehearsals of a play will take. So the actors are usually presented with a *fait accompli* as regards the basic design and interpretation of the play – its fundamental 'concept' – as they gather for their first read-throughs of a script. John Russell Brown describes this concept approach to staging Shakespeare: 'Besides being "just the servant of the play" and the organizer of its production, the director functions as an interpreter. Like a film camera, his job is to get us to "see" the play through his eyes. If necessary, he will enlarge, underscore, repeat and eliminate, until no one could fail to see what he is getting at, even if in the process other possibilities are wholly lost to sight.'[3] Brown is very much concerned about those 'other possibilities', but for the moment let us stay with the director's function as interpreter and the way he or she thus provides coherence to a production. For indeed there are many 'possibilities' in any Shakespearean text, rich as they are in ambiguity and complexity. Modern directors frequently see their job, however, as having to choose from among those possibilities one, and only one, interpretation so that their productions can achieve unity and coherence.

Of course, not all interpretations are successful. When the director wrenches the script from the received text, distorting it for some end, political or social or otherwise, we may question the legitimacy of the interpretation. Coherence may have been achieved, but at what cost? With Thomas Clayton, we need to ponder the 'dialectic' between the author's intention and the relevance for modern audiences, or the distinction between 'meaning' and 'significance.'[4] A director may have a brilliant idea for interpreting a play, say *Twelfth Night*, and it may work very well in the theatre. But we may question at the end, Was it Shakespeare?

[75]

Thus Irving Wardle questions a recent RSC production:

> Quite a bit of poison has been seeping into this play over the past few years, but John Caird's [production] is the first I have seen that projects *Twelfth Night* as an all-out dark comedy. This is good news not only for jaded old spectators who have seen the piece too often. There is a limit to the amount of fun that can be extracted from the drinking scene and the permutations of Malvolio's letter in a play that was never more than intermittently uproarious. And there is everything to be said for muting the comedy for once and giving full attention to the central matter of the illusion and frenzies of love.[5]

Wardle approves of the production, mainly as a fresh interpretation that helps focus on central issues in the play, issues that are not unShakespearean at all. But John Russell Brown takes quite a different view of Buzz Goodbody's production of *King John* in 1970, where the characters marched about like toy soldiers, repeated phrases in 'parrot-like' chorus, prayed in unison, etc. 'The director wished to stress the repetitions, self-satisfaction and self-interest of politics, and she did so with wearying completeness. The suffering, uncertainty, passion and moral considerations, so often suggested by the text, were crowded out, submerged in what the director was telling us.'[6]

Political interpretations are by no means uncommon today among productions of Shakespeare's plays. One recalls Michael Edwards' anti-war *Henry IV, Part One*, at Santa Cruz in 1984, or the Theatre Company's production of *The Tempest* in 1982 that questioned Prospero's 'colonization' of his island and equated his 'usurpation' with those attempted or achieved by Alonzo's shipmates.[7] Political interpretation can thus be more subtle than, say, the adaptation of *Macbeth* into the frankly parodic *Macbird*. Directors are hardly above exploiting Shakespearean texts for political ends. Laurence Olivier's film of *Henry V* was a great nationalistic triumph at a time (1944) when Britain needed the kind of inspiration the film provided. But to emphasize the heroic aspects of King Henry and thus exalt him as the great mirror for all Christian kings he was, in part, intended to appear, Olivier needed to cut other, more ambiguous aspects of his character. He accordingly played down the qualities that linked him to his father, Henry IV, that 'vile politician', as Hotspur calls him in *Henry IV, Part One*. What emerged was what was wanted; it had coherence, unity, and great public appeal. It still does – except for those who question the reductivism to which Olivier submitted Shakespeare's text in finding the coherence and interpretation that he wanted.[8]

Not only the English history plays are subject to political interpretation. The Roman tragedies are as well. *Julius Caesar* has been a prime candidate for many years, at least as far back as before World War II, where the resemblances between Caesar and Mussolini became irresistible to directors. Caesar is still occasionally played as a modern-day fascist, with or without a toga, as in the BBC-TV production, where Charles Gray as Caesar struck poses and thrust out his jaw to make the connection with Mussolini unmistakable.[9] Sometimes it is unnecessary to slant a production to get a desired – or unexpected – political effect; just the staging of a particular play at a particular time may be enough to bring forth a political issue inherent in the text. Ian McKellen reports on a surprising audience response to *Richard II* in 1969 when the RSC toured the play in Czechoslovakia. The audience was overwhelmed and ended up weeping audibly, as they identified powerfully with the stage action in the light of their own recent political experience.[10] And Michael Kahn notes apropos of *Julius Caesar* and the American presidential election in 1972 that he could find no candidate to vote for. 'Although my sympathies were for George McGovern I thought he would make a terrible President, and my sympathies were not for Richard Nixon but I thought he would probably make a better President than George McGovern although he was a despicable human being. I found politics to be an almost insoluble problem to deal with, and I found that to be true in *Julius Caesar*.'[11]

Antony and Cleopatra and *Coriolanus* similarly contain strong political themes, although they are also about other important issues. A director may choose to emphasize, and perhaps distort, a political issue to achieve a kind of unity in a production and in so doing exploit the text for purposes of his or her own. As Robert Speaight comments, 'No play lends itself more easily to a political *parti-pris* than *Coriolanus*'. He then describes the political passions aroused by Copeau's production in Paris, 1932-34, when the anti-democratic sentiments in the play received a standing ovation and the curtain had to be lowered twenty times during the performance. The production consistently roused political emotions so violent that in February 1934 it had to be temporarily suspended. In March, when it resumed, the anti-democratic tirades of Jean

Hervé, who played Coriolanus, again brought the house down. Shortly afterwards, Speaight continues, *Coriolanus* was produced in Moscow at the Maly Theatre as 'a drama of individualism' to show 'a superman who had detached himself from the people and betrayed them.'[12]

Social issues may also be exploited. Recently, *Romeo and Juliet* seems to have become a vehicle for issues of this kind, as in Michael Bogdanov's RSC production of the play in 1986. Set in the present, complete with motorcycles and an Alfa Romeo sports car (hence the production's nickname, 'Alfa Romeo and Juliet'), the play was cut and slanted to emphasize the decadence of the nouveau riche, as the Capulets were portrayed. In such a social-climbing, crass society as this Verona was made to appear, the innocent love of Romeo and Juliet stood no chance. At the end, the gilded statues erected by their parents did less to honor them than to drive home the production's point about the wasted lives. Everything inherently wrong with the society was underscored by the 'media event' that was the concluding scene, in which the opening Prologue became the Epilogue.

Michael Kahn's production of *Romeo and Juliet* the same year at The Shakespeare Theatre at the Folger was less drastically altered to fit its social intention, but there was one, nevertheless. Perhaps if one arrived late at the theatre and did not read the program notes, one might have missed what it was, for the production was done in a Renaissance setting and played 'straight'. But if one looked at page 6 of the program and read the article entitled, '*Romeo and Juliet:* A Dramatic Approach to Prevention of Youth Suicide', one might have had a rather different theatrical experience. Certainly in this context Juliet's contemplation of suicide at the end of Act III (after she has been pressured to marry Count Paris) and moments later when she talks with Friar Lawrence brings a new and deeper perspective to the play. The didactic intention was pressed home in two pre-performance discussions conducted by representatives of the Youth Suicide National Center and members of the cast on November 12 and 22. In addition, the program note advises, 'a workshop and materials for school personnel will be provided to teachers to assist them in dealing with the issue of suicide as it arises during class discussions of *Romeo and Juliet*'. The announced purpose of all this was not only 'to help our young people to experience the beauty and sadness of this drama', but also to 'understand that the tragedy of youth suicide results in wasted lives and grieving survivors'. So that the audience would be conscious of this emphasis from the beginning, regardless of the program note, the production opened with a tableau of Romeo and Juliet dead in each other's arms, just as they appear later in Act V.

So much for ideology, political or social or both. While it can provide unity for a production, it may do so by overriding other aspects of the play or losing them altogether. John Russell Brown vehemently objects to this approach to Shakespeare and advocates a much greater freedom for interpretation, even during actual performance, on the part of the actors. In his view, this would bring performance closer to Elizabethan staging, when there was less time for rehearsals and much less in the way of settings, lighting, and properties to worry about. As he imagines them, Shakespeare's plays in their first performances must have been like a 'happening', or a football match, in which 'the quality of play was part of the play'.

> Because almost nothing besides the words was 'fixed,' as we say, [the actor's] contribution could and would change from day to day, according to his state of mind and feeling, his reactions to life and events outside the theatre. Tempo would change; different parts of his role would be pointed according to his own experience of living and his own fantasies, and its impression be strengthened in response to his growing acquaintance with the play and with his fellow actors. He would be influenced, too, by his audience, which was not separated from him by darkness and could support or ignore him according to their changing concerns, the time of year, or the political climate. Every play, despite the elaborate words which were its controlling element, must have been precarious in performance, and every performance must have been different from another.[13]

One might expect to find not much unity and perhaps precious little coherence in a performance of this kind, especially since the actors never had the full text of the play in their hands. They were given only their own parts and their cues. They of course had to listen well and to follow the instructions of the author or whoever took charge, but clearly no 'director', as we know it, was present. It is remarkable, under these circumstances, how many plays were successful, at least in Elizabethan terms, where long runs consisted of perhaps five or six performances – not scores or hundreds and an international tour afterwards! Audiences loved a play with good rhetoric and sufficient action, and possibly they were not troubled by considerations of unity and coherence, at any rate as we conceive them.

But this is not really Brown's point. His point is to free Shakespearean representation from the 'fixed' quality of contemporary productions, so that actors are more at liberty to discover the complexities of the text and reveal them to themselves and their audience, *even in the act of performing*. Everyone who has had any experience in the theatre knows that often in rehearsals things happen that can, for a moment anyway, transfigure the playing of a scene or a whole play. The actors suddenly catch fire or penetrate more deeply than ever into what is most essential in what they are doing, and bring it out fully alive. It can sometimes happen in performance. Brown tells the story, probably apocryphal, of Olivier's *Othello* at the National Theatre when, some time after it had opened, Olivier's performance 'seemed to grow in power and danger'. Others caught fire from him and topped their previous renditions, giving the play new freshness and excitement. Audience response was overwhelming. Afterwards, when Maggie Smith rushed to congratulate Olivier, she found him a picture of despair. He knew very well what had happened, but he did not know why.[14] The play had been 'fixed', its lines of interpretation clearly drawn, but in performance a new spontaneity had taken over, inspiriting the actors and transforming their playing.

Perhaps this spontaneity emanating from well-prepared actors leads to the ideal performance that, like most ideals, is realized rarely. Nevertheless, it is a goal worth working toward. It provides for diversity within unity and keeps productions fresh and alive. Richard Burton is said to have had several different ways of performing the Nunnery Scene in *Hamlet*, directed by John Gielgud in 1964, and the cast never knew which one he would choose on any given night. Nor did he until the scene arrived and he had to play it.[15] In other respects, the play was 'set', or 'fixed', and retained what coherence it had; Burton's various renditions of the Nunnery Scene did not destroy it.

Finally, we need to distinguish between Brown's call for 'free Shakespeare' and Stanislavski's 'through line of action'. They are by no means incompatible ideas for producing Shakespeare's plays. On the contrary, they are complementary. In calling for a through line of action, Stanislavski insists upon actors maintaining a clear perspective not only on how their roles develop over the course of the play, but also on how all of their roles fit together.

As he explains to one of the student actors in *Building a Character*, 'You need that rapid glance into the past and the future in order to make a proper estimate of the present action, and the better you sense its relationship to the whole play the easier it will be for you to focus the full extent of your attention to it.[16] The through line of action provides the consistency of point of view, the thread on which the various scenes are strung, but it need not rigidify the acting or the interpretation of the whole so that new insights and representations are prohibited. It derives from what Stanislavski later refers to as the 'inner life' of the play and its characters, or the 'fundamental core, the idea which impelled the writer, the poet, to produce his composition'.[17]

In Shakespeare's plays, this inner life or fundamental core is never single or simple; it is various and complex. The questions then become for the audience: How much of the essential complexity of the play has the production realized? Has the play been reduced to a single or simplistic rendering of the text, to prove some point or other, or to make the play more immediately accessible to a contemporary audience? Have the actors in their portrayals released the richness of their roles, complementing each other in ways that provide for a full-bodied representation of the whole; or have they struck for the direct, easy, sure representation that fits some predetermined structure? We crave unity and want coherence, but what about complexity and ambiguity? Is the performance giving them to us also, we may ask; or are we being somehow short-changed, bowled over by scenic splendour or individual performances or clever stage business and musical effects?

I should have liked to see a performance of *The Tempest* presented by the Festival Theatre, Stratford, Canada, in 1982. Although as Ralph Berry describes it, the production had serious flaws, it was also remarkable for its excellences.[18] Len Cariou's young, angry Prospero did not convey the complexity of his role, and Miles Potter's Caliban was undistinguished. Ariel had some fine moments, however, as in his dialogue with Prospero about compassion for the captive malefactors. But Nicholas Pennel as Stephano the drunken butler was apparently worth the price of admission: according to Berry, he had an interior life that the others lacked; he was 'a Gloucester or Iago in the making. . . appallingly aware of the power that chance had placed in his hands'. Pennell's understanding of his role – and of the play – was reflected in his acting, which had great conviction. Costumes and effects, as in the

Banquet Scene and the Masque, were inventive and illuminating; they also demonstrated that the director, John Hirsch, had basically a good idea for his production, which unfortunately fulfilled neither his expectations nor the play's richness. An uneven production, then, but one not totally unsatisfying, and the audience could learn from it.

To conclude: We may experience many different kinds of satisfaction when we are in the theatre and afterwards, when we contemplate what we have witnessed. Should we settle for the easy satisfaction a finely crafted production creates, or demand the more difficult, less immediately satisfying – because more intellectually and emotionally stimulating – experience that performances of Shakespeare's plays can also provide? Directors may continue to ride their hobby-horses, and designers may continue to dominate the large theatrical companies. But need we accept everything they offer? In the last analysis, it may be worth sacrificing unity and coherence, if they come at the cost of a distorting ideology imposed upon the play (and therefore upon us), in favor of a less unified and coherent production. If such a production sets us thinking more deeply about the issues that lie at the heart of Shakespeare's creation, should we prefer it, even though the production has only partially revealed the play's inner core, but honestly and richly? Is it not for that, after all, that the serious theatregoer goes to see Shakespeare performed?

But we need not acquiesce in either/or choices. Surely, Shakespeare's plays can offer us both, coherence and complexity, when well and competently staged. For some of the plays, like *Hamlet*, which defy finding coherence because their composition rejects it, that may be too much to expect, and the temptation for directors may be to impose on them a coherence they do not have. But for most of the plays, if presented to us honestly and directly, coherence and complexity are not an impossible goal, one that can be and often is achieved by dedicated and capable Shakespeare companies all over the world.

EPILOGUE

The enjoyment of Shakespeare

The enjoyment of Shakespeare's plays in performance begins with the excitement of anticipation. Finding what's on, checking the cast and direction, buying the tickets all contribute to the anticipation of pleasure. The pleasure is of several kinds: good acting, well-designed and tasteful sets, sensitive verse speaking, appropriate music and other effects, including lighting. We also expect an interpretation or rendition of the play that will bring Shakespeare closer to us, make him accessible in ways we had not experienced before so that we can see and hear more clearly than ever what he is about.

This kind of enjoyment presupposes an approach or attitude that this book has stressed from the beginning. To enjoy Shakespeare today we require an open mind and a receptive sensibility. Fixed ideas about how a play should be performed can be and usually are self-defeating. Inevitably they lead to disappointment and disapproval. This does not mean that when we enter the theatre we must leave our critical intelligence behind. Not at all. Serious theatregoers will also bring with them as much information as possible along with their inquiring, or open, minds. But the information – about Shakespeare, his age, the plays – need not set or fix an attitude or expectation any more than it should stifle the intellect's searching attitude.

Shakespeare can speak to us as powerfully and as delightfully today as he did to his countrymen four hundred years ago. But we need to listen and watch more attentively than – certainly as imaginatively as – the theatregoers of London did in 1595 or 1602 or 1610. Therein lies the key to the enjoyment of Shakespeare. Modern technology and other benefits today can enhance the enjoyment, but they can also cripple it, if they are allowed to take over. As old Adam warns Orlando in *As You Like It,* our virtues may become 'sanctified and holy traitors' and betray us in matters of deepest consequence. This is where the theatregoer's critical intelligence comes into play, analyzing and evaluating the contributions to a production that modern technology, historical and psychological research, and other manifestations of our culture have made. We need not accept the contributions, such as they are, but neither should we reject them out of hand.

When we arrive at the theatre, then, our expectations may be great but should not be rigid. Since Shakespeare's plays resist definitive interpretations or productions, we need to remain open to the performance we are about to witness. We may have studied the text in advance, or we may not have. If we have, we will be better prepared to note the changes in the text and to assess those changes and their relation to the overall interpretation of the play. If we have not, the production may still speak to us, but we will be in a less advantageous position to judge whether what we are seeing is 'Shakespeare' or some kind of adaptation (if, that is, the question has any importance for us). We may enjoy the sets and costume design, regardless of the period, and then determine for ourselves whether they add to or detract from the performance. Are we in designer's theatre or actor's theatre? Do the sets and other aspects of design overwhelm the production, or enhance it?

Similarly, we can enjoy the various bits of stage business without checking to see if Shakespeare (or someone else in his company) wrote them into the stage directions. But again, we can ask the question: do these bits of stage business reveal something we might not otherwise have seen, or do they seem to have been introduced for their own sake, to demonstrate the cleverness of the actors or director? Music may be enhancing in ways similar to set designs, or it may be intrusive, insistently calling attention to itself and away from the player's actions or the lines they are speaking. It need not be the original music Shakespeare's company used, certainly not if the set design is of a very different period. But like everything else in the production, it should blend in and become part of the whole. In the final analysis, we look to the acting and directing and inquire whether they have given us an original and acceptable interpretation of the text, one that informs us as well as moves us. Without question, it is an actor's virtuosity or charisma – his or her ability to captivate an audience – to which we respond most directly and completely in any performance. Nevertheless, we need to be aware of the gimmicks that even the finest and most accomplished actors may adopt. We need to look instead for a clear, perceptive, and revealing interpretation of character as transmitted powerfully through the actor's understanding of the text, grasp of subtext, and competence in speaking Shakespeare's lines. Whatever the stage design, whatever period the play is set in, whatever the effects that are introduced to enhance the production, we respond first and finally to the characters, language, and action in Shakespeare's plays.

It is the director's job to bring all this together in some meaningful whole, being careful that neither the spirit nor the essentials – the 'inner core' – of Shakespeare's play is violated. Among the essentials are a respect for the play's basic dramatic structure, the proper interplay of character and action, and an overall interpretation that fits the text and does not distort or pervert it. An able director can mold the production into a seamless fabric so that whatever cuts have been made are not noticeable, and the actors perform as a true ensemble. This seamless quality is something else that we respond to as an audience, perhaps less consciously than to other aspects of a production, but none the less surely. It is another way of defining coherence. But we should be ready to sacrifice even this pleasure for other pleasures, those that may bring us greater insights into the plays and into our world through the plays.

In short, if the through line of the action is firm, if the interpretation of the play grips us and provides good insight into the language and meaning of the play, if the subordinate aspects of the production remain truly subordinate and do not usurp attention, our experience may be commensurate to the effort of the acting company. And it is there – in the language and grace and competence of fine actors moving in well-designed space – that we will find the pleasures and the rewards that are rightly ours in the enjoyment of Shakespeare's plays in performance.

NOTES

Chapter I

1 Cp. J. C. Maxwell, 'Shakespeare: The Middle Plays', *A Guide to English Literature: The Age of Shakespeare*, ed. Boris Ford (Baltimore: Penguin Books, 1955), II, 213.

2 See Michael Warren and Gary Taylor, eds., *The Division of the Kingdoms* (Oxford: Clarendon Press, 1983). The new Oxford edition of the complete works, edited by Stanley Wells and Gary Taylor, prints both versions of *King Lear* as separate texts.

3 Albert B. Weiner discusses the piracy question at length in his Introduction to *Hamlet: The First Quarto, 1603* (Great Neck, NY: Barron's Educational Series, 1962), pp. 7-45.

4 See, e.g., Philip Edwards' discussion in his New Cambridge Shakespeare edition of the play (Cambridge University Press, 1985), pp. 8-32, esp. p. 20.

5 *Shakespeare's Occasional Plays* (London: Edward Arnold, 1965).

6 Grigori Kozintsev, *Shakespeare: Time and Conscience*, tr. Joyce Vining (New York: Hill and Wang, 1966), p. 215.

7 Ibid., p. 215.

8 In *The Triple Bond: Plays, Mainly Shakespearean, in Performance*, ed. Joseph G. Price (University Park: Pennsylvania State University Press, 1975), pp. 30-49.

9 'Theatrical Shakespearegresses at the Guthrie and Elsewhere: Notes on "Legitimate Production"', *New Literary History*, 17 (1985-86), 533.

10 In Ralph Berry, *On Directing Shakespeare: Interviews with Contemporary Directors* (London: Croom Helm, 1977), p. 71. Cp. Peter Hall's remark on cutting *Hamlet* in *Peter Hall's Diaries*, ed. John Goodwin (London: Hamish Hamilton, 1983), p. 177: 'But we still cut the text like barbarians. Do we know what we cut? And don't we normally cut either to fit some preconceived theory for the production, or because we simply can't make the passage work?'

11 Cp. Berry's comments on this play in his Introduction, p. 18.

12 Stewart and Suchet discuss their portrayals in John Barton's *Playing Shakespeare* (London: Methuen, 1984), pp. 170-180. See also the discussion below in Chapter III, 'Finding the Characters'.

13 Laurence Olivier says his portrayal of Shylock owed much to the figure of Benjamin Disraeli. See his discussion of the role in his book, *On Acting* (New York: Simon and Schuster: 1986), pp. 172-186.

14 Cp. Patrick J. Sullivan, 'Strumpet Wind – The National Theatre's *Merchant of Venice*', *Educational Theatre Journal*, 26 (March 1974), 31-44. Sullivan's otherwise excellent account of the production notes the cut in I.iii but few of the others. He has very high praise for Olivier's Shylock and Miller's direction, and concludes: 'With a production like this one, performance becomes itself a critical act' (p. 44). Cp. Clayton's discussion of the possible stage endings of *The Merchant*, pp. 531-533.

15 The New York *Times'* regular critics, Clive Barnes and Mel Gussow, thoroughly applauded this production, but Harris Green in a later review thought Shakespeare's play had been obliterated. See the *Times* for August 18, November 13, 1972, and

January 14, 1973.

16 A Facsimile Published by Cornmarket Press from the Copy in the Birmingham Shakespeare Library (London, 1969). In his Introduction to the Cornmarket Press facsimile of *Hamlet: J. P. Kemble 1800* (London, 1971), T. J. B. Spencer indicates that the 1676 edition was the text most probably prepared by Davenant and played by Betterton from 1661 to 1709. Among the omissions he notes are the Norwegian embassy of Voltimand and Cornelius, the scene with Reynaldo, most of the lines concerning Fortinbras, Polonius' advice to Laertes, much of Hamlet's first speech to the Ghost, most of the Pyrrhus episode, and Hamlet's advice to the Players.

17 The New Cambridge Shakespeare, under the general editorship of Philip Brockbank, and the New Oxford Shakespeare, under the general editorship of Stanley Wells, make a serious attempt to include more about staging in the running commentaries for the plays in their series.

18 The lines also appear in the other authoritative text, the folio of 1623, but not in Q1, the 'Bad' Quarto of 1603. The Reynaldo episode appears in all three versions, although much curtailed in Q1, where the characters' names are also different.

19 The text, published by Mayflower Books (New York, 1980), is that of Peter Alexander. Cuts are judiciously made throughout; no major scenes or characters are omitted, and usually only a few lines here and there are cut, the most notable being, perhaps, II.ii.471-491, from the First Player's speech describing Pyrrhus' attack on Priam.

20 Staged at the Shakespeare Theatre at the Folger. He also began the play with a tableau of Romeo and Juliet dead in the tomb during the Prologue. One of the most famous interpolations of a scene was Henry Irving's portrayal, in pantomime, of Shylock's return after dining with Bassanio to find Jessica gone in *The Merchant of Venice*.

21 'S. Franco Zeffirelli's *Romeo and Juliet*', *Shakespeare Survey* 15, ed. Allardyce Nicoll (Cambridge: Cambridge U. P., 1962), p. 153. Reprinted in *Shakespeare's Plays in Performance* (Baltimore: Penguin Books, 1969), p. 191.

22 See Jay L. Halio, 'Zeffirelli's *Romeo and Juliet:* The Camera versus the Text', *Literature/Film Quarterly*, 5 (Fall 1977), 322-325.

23 Among the most famous additions is Colley Cibber's 'Off with his head. So much for Buckingham' – a line so beloved by actors playing Richard III that it may still be heard in modern productions of Shakespeare's history play. Cibber's adaptation of *Richard III* held the stage well into the nineteenth century and may have influenced Laurence Olivier's recreation of the role.

24 This was not original to Olivier's production. See Arthur Colby Sprague and J. C. Trewin, *Shakespeare's Plays Today* (Columbia: University of South Carolina Press, 1970), p. 61. They attribute the innovation to John Burrell's production at the New Theatre, September 1944.

25 See Jack J. Jorgens, 'Shakespeare on Film and Television', in *Shakespeare: His World, His Work, His Influence*, ed. John Andrews (New York: Scribner's, 1985), p. 690. For a full discussion of filmed versions of Shakespeare, see Jorgens' book, *Shakespeare on Film* (Bloomington: Indiana University Press, 1977).

Chapter II

1 In a seminar on 'The Royal Shakespeare Company: Retrospect and Prospect', Shakespeare Association of American, Cambridge, Mass., April 1984.

2 See J. M. Nosworthy, *Shakespeare's Occasional Plays. Their Origin and Transmission* (London: Edward Arnold, 1965).

3 See Stanley Wells, 'Shakespeare on the English Stage', and Charles Shattuck, 'Shakespeare in the Theater: the United States and Canada', in *William Shakespeare: His World, His Work, and His Influence*, ed. John Andrews (New York: Scribner's, 1985), III, 603-661.

4 Cp. John Barton, *Playing Shakespeare* (London: Methuen, 1984), p. 186: 'I think the great question about changing the period of a play is "Does it help unlock some-

thing that is truly in the text, or does it distort the play?" '

5 Quoted in David Selbourne, *The Making of A Midsummer Night's Dream* (London: Methuen, 1982), p. 43. Brook also told his actors that the 'old traditions of *A Midsummer Night's Dream* set up echoes which prevented anyone doing it directly', i.e. approaching the text afresh (p. 53).

6 Benedict Nightingale considered Brook's *Dream* 'perverse': see 'Dream 2001', *The New Statesman*, 80 (4 Sept. 1970), 281 for the Stratford performance, and 'Tripping Gaily', *The New Statesman* 81 (18 June 1971), 858-859 for the one at London's Alwych Theatre.

7 Cp. Gareth Lloyd Evans, 'Shakespeare in Stratford and London, 1981', *Shakespeare Quarterly*, 33 (Summer 1982), 187-188: 'This production was, arguably, a mix-up amalgam of Brook's theatricality, Kott's misguided intellectuality, the RSC's own contemporary obsession with Dickens. . . , and a few personal quiddities of the director'.

8 In 1986 the RSC staged the *Dream* Bill Alexander directed, and the set was designed by William Dudley. The movement back to the nineteenth century apparently continues, as the staging was all Arthur Rackham and Lewis Carroll.

9 In *On Directing Shakespeare*, ed. Ralph Berry (New York: Barnes & Noble, 1977), pp. 124-126.

10 Ibid,. p. 20

11 In a comment upon a draft of this chapter.

12 See Brook in *On Directing Shakespeare*, p. 125, and Barton, p. 185.

13 So successful was the television production, that the stage version closed a week later.

14 Cp. Ian McKellen on John Barton's production of the play, set in the last days of the Empire in India: 'I thought that [setting] released my view of the play enormously. It did what you always have to do with that play, which is to to provide a strict social set-up to explain why Beatrice is the woman she is and why Benedick is the man he is, and why they are somehow, despite themselves, trapped in a set of conventions' (*Playing Shakespeare*, p. 186).

15 Cp. John Elsom's review, 'Bless My Soul', *The Listener*, 106 (23 April 1981), 582: 'It [Rudman's treatment of the play] is potentially exciting and radical, answering many questions posed by this fascinating and troublesome play, casting new light on them and transforming the tone from sombre tragi-comedy towards that of a less flippant Candide. The failures come when Rudman lacks the courage of his inspiration, either because he has not thought through the implications or because he was reluctant to carry them out.' See also Thomas Clayton's discussion of this production in 'Theatrical Shakespearegresses at the Guthrie and Elsewhere: Notes on "Legitimate Production"' *New Literary History*, 17 (1985-86), 523524.

16 See Dessen's detailed review of the production (to which I am indebted for these comments and descriptions) in 'Staging Shakespeare's History Plays in 1984: A Tale of Three Henrys', *Shakespeare Quarterly*, 36 (1985), 75-78.

Chapter III

1 Cp. John Russell Brown's discussion of the different ways these words may be spoken on stage, in *Free Shakespeare* (London: Heinemann, 1974), p. 64.

2 Antony Sher has written at length about his experience in his book, *Year of the King: An Actor's Diary and Sketchbook* (London: Chatto & Windus, 1985; reprinted in paperback by Methuen).

3 Richard David's comparison of two productions of *1 Henry IV* in *Shakespeare in the Theatre* (Cambridge, 1978) is instructive. See especially his discussion of the relationship between King Henry and his son as developed in III.ii, pp. 200-1. In one production (Stratford, 1951), father and son are hopelessly unlike each other and therefore find it impossible to communicate effectively; in the other (Stratford, 1975), father and son are very close in both character and feeling, despite their temporary estrangement. David concludes: 'The contrast demonstrates. . . that there is no one

way, unique and ideal, of presenting a play, and that the method and even some shades of the meaning must vary according to the medium, that is the actors, by which the communication is to be made.'

4 J. L. Styan, *Shakespeare in Performance: All's Well That Ends Well* (Manchester: Manchester University Press, 1984), pp. 16-20.

5 *Players of Shakespeare*, p. 153.

6 Ibid., p. 157. Recall that Gemma Jones also played the lead in *The Duchess of Duke Street* television series.

7 Ibid., p. 158.

8 *Playing Shakespeare* (London: Methuen, 1984), p. 180.

9 Cp. Norman Rabkin's essay on the play in *Shakespeare and the Problem of Meaning* (Chicago: University of Chicago Pres, 1981).

10 *Playing Shakespeare*, p. 171.

11 Compare Laurence Olivier's portrayal in Jonathan Miller's National Theatre production for still another approach to Shylock's character and its representation on the contemporary stage, as discussed in Chapter I. Stewart expands on his conception of Shylock in *Players of Shakespeare*, pp. 11-28.

12 See Leo Kirschbaum, '"Banquo and Edgar: Character or Function?' *Essays in Criticism*, 7 (1957), 1-21.

13 *Shakespeare and the Energies of Drama* (Princeton: Princeton University Press, 1972), p. 97.

14 William A. Ringler, Jr., believes that Armin was too old by now to play the Fool and took Edgar's part instead, since it requires multiple roles and Armin was good at that. Ringler argues that the boy actor who played Cordelia also played the Fool. See 'Shakespeare and His Actors: Some Remarks on *King Lear*', in *Shakespeare's Art from a Comparative Perspective*, ed. W. M. Aycock (Lubbock: Texas Tech Press, 1981), pp. 188-190. The idea that the parts of Cordelia and the Fool were doubled has been much debated; see also Richard Abrams, 'The Doubling of Cordelia and Lear's Fool', *Texas Studies in Language and Literature*, 27 (1985), 354-368.

15 In the nineteenth century Macready actually used an actress, Priscilla Horton, in the role of the Fool. Other actor-managers followed this innovation, but the actresses did not play both Cordelia and the Fool. See Carol Jones Carlisle, *Shakespeare from the Greenroom* (Chapel Hill: University of North Carolina Press, 1969), p. 313.

16 The RSC production in Stratford-upon-Avon in 1982 opened with a tableau that had Cordelia and the Fool seated on the throne in midstage with cords around their necks, emphasizing their relationship and foreshadowing the line, 'And my poor fool is hang'd' (V.iii.306). But the Fool was not hanged in that production; actually, he was killed by Lear, who mistakes him for Regan in the mock trial scene (III.vi).

17 *Shakespeare in the Greenroom*, p. 395.

Chapter IV

1 Although this term was not used in the previous chapter – if only because it deserves a chapter of its own – its importance was frequently suggested, as for example in Gemma Jones's reference to her 'interior monologues'. Establishing a subtext is an essential part of an actor's motivation for the character being played.

2 *Shakespeare's Plays in Performance*, p. 69.

3 See V.i.126-129 and note Philip McGuire's analysis of the situation in *Speechless Dialect: Shakespeare's Open Silences* (Berkeley: University of California Press, 1985), pp. 38-44.

4 Quoted by Judith Cook, *Shakespeare's Players* (London: Harrap, 1983), p. 71.

5 Cp. Hugh Griffith's conception of the part, as Michael Greenwald describes it in *Directions by Indirections: John Barton of the Royal Shakespeare Company* (Newark: University of Delaware Press, 1985), p. 59. Citing a programme note, Greenwald says that Griffith's non-romantic Falstaff showed what the good life in Eastcheap really implied: 'deceit, murder, swindling, chaos, vanity, viciousness – an attack on the basic and precious laws which bind men together'.

6 *Shakespeare's Players*, p. 72.

7 Ibid., p. 94.

8 Tyrone Guthrie, *In Various Directions: A View of Theatre* (New York: Macmillan, 1965), pp. 90-91.

9 Guthrie, p. 92. Although he does not specifically use the term subtext, Guthrie's comments suggest that it is this which he has in mind: '. . . it is apparent that the text alone is only a limited guide. "Over and above", and "between the lines", not in them, lies the real meaning' (p. 91).

10 'The Duke and Isabella on the Modern Stage', *The Triple Bond*, ed. Joseph G. Price (University Park and London: Pennsylvania State University Press, 1975), pp. 149-169.

11 See Nevill Coghill, 'Comic Form in *Measure for Measure*', *Shakespeare Survey*, 8 (1955), 14-27.

12 Williamson, p. 168, cites Anne Barton's programme note for the production: 'We do not know how Isabella reacts to her sovereign's extraordinarily abrupt offer of marriage in the final moments of the play, because she says nothing to him in reply. It is at least possible that this silence is one of dismay.' She also cites the reviewer in *The Listener* who saw an even stronger response from this 'feminist' Isabella, who had 'silent rage written all over her high forehead and stubborn chin' and stood alone downstage at the end 'glaring at the audience'. Cp. Greenwald, p. 103, who comments on the ambiguous aspects of Barton's ending, which may have been prompted by Marvin Rosenberg's essay, 'Shakespeare's Fantastic Trick: *Measure for Measure*', first presented at the Shakespeare Institute in Stratford-upon-Avon and then published in *Sewanee Review*, 80 (1972), 51-72.

13 *Changing Styles in Shakespeare* (London: George Allen & Unwin, 1981), p. 44.

14 Williamson, p. 169; cited also by Berry, p. 44.

15 Berry, p. 45.

16 Craig Raine, *The New Statesman*, 22 August 1975; cited by Berry, p. 45.

17 See also McGuire, pp. 63-96, who discusses not only Isabella's 'open silence', but those of several other characters in the final scene, including Claudio and Juliet, Barnardine, and Angelo. He also analyzes the implications of the staging, particularly the blocking, of the scene to show how the relationships of erotic and filial love are concluded.

18 Laurence Senelik, *Gordon Craig's Moscow 'Hamlet'* (Westport, CT: 1982), p. 64; quoted by Joyce Vining Morgan, *Stanislavski's Encounter with Shakespeare* (Ann Arbor, MI: UMI Research Press, 1984), p. 91.

19 See Francis Fergusson, *The Idea of a Theater* (Princeton: Princeton University Press, 1949; rpt. Anchor Books, 1953), p. 135 (references are to the reprint). Fergusson's discussion of Jones's interpretation on pp. 122-123 is important, but so is his entire chapter devoted to the play.

20 Guthrie, p. 78. Guthrie regards Hamlet as 'not only highly intelligent, but also a resolute and capable man, rendered irresolute and incapable by self-conflict, by qualms of conscience, only in the single matter of avenging his father's death by the murder of his uncle'. He believes Jones's interpretation is convincing but offers little that can be expressed theatrically. Using analogies from two episodes in Queen Elizabeth's experience, Guthrie concludes with Salvador de Madariaga that Hamlet did not fail to act; he postponed action until the moment for action had clearly been revealed, as it was in the final scene. See pp. 79-82.

21 Shakespeare's history plays tend to be tragedies or comedies, but usually a combination of both genres.

22 *Building a Character*, p. 169.

Chapter V

1 See John Barton, *Playing Shakespeare* (London: Methuen, 1984), pp. 8-9.

2 *The Janus of the Poets* (New York: Macmillan; Cambridge: Cambridge University Press, 1935), pp. 42-43.

3 The punctuation in most modern editions is not Shakespeare's. The sixteenth- and seventeenth-century texts sometimes reflect the dramatic pointing of speeches, which was very light by modern standards and followed different principles.

4 Barton, p. 50.

5 Barton, p. 51.

6 *Prefaces to Shakespeare* (Princeton: Princeton University Press, 1946), I, 12.

7 *Players of Shakespeare*, ed. Philip Brockbank (Cambridge: Cambridge University Press, 1985), pp. 121-122.

8 Cp. Granville-Barker, pp. 13-14: 'If we are to make Shakespeare our own again we must all be put to a little trouble about it. We must recapture as far as may be his lost meanings. . . . The tunes that he writes to, the whole great art of his music-making, we can master. Actors can train their ears and tongues and can train our ears to it. . . No art is ever lost while the means to it survive. Our faculties rust by disuse and by misuse are coarsened, but they quickly recover delight in a beautiful thing.'

9 Richard David compares Shakespeare's verse here with an entirely different style used earlier in the play at II.i.11-15. See pp. 79-80 for his discussion of Shakespeare's so-called unevenness of style and his dramatic method.

10 See Helge Kökeritz, *Shakespeare's Pronunciation* (New Haven: Yale University Press, 1953), p. 91.

11 For Hamlet's puns here and elsewhere, see M. M. Mahood, *Shakespeare's Wordplay* (London: Methuen, 1957), p. 114 ff. This is still the best book on the subject and well worth reading for anyone interested in Shakespeare's use of ambiguity.

12 Ibid., pp. 140-3.

13 *Jure ye* is probably a nonce formation simply intended as a nonsense play on *grandjurors*. See Kökeritz, p. 76.

14 *Shakespeare's Wordplay*, p. 60.

15 In *The Well Wrought Urn* (New York: Harcourt, Brace: 1947).

16 Caroline Spurgeon's pioneering work, *Shakespeare's Imagery and What It Tells Us* (Cambridge: Cambridge University Press, 1935), led the way to many subsequent studies, chief among them Donald Stauffer's *Shakespeare's World of Images: The Development of His Moral Ideas* (1949) and Wolfgang Clemen's *The Development of Shakespeare's Imagery* (1951).

Chapter VI

1 Cp. Ann Pasternak Slater, *Shakespeare the Director* (Sussex: Harvester Press; New Jersey: Barnes & Noble, 1982), pp. 60-61

2 In *Richard III*, II.i, for example, Catesby is listed among those who enter with the King and Queen, but he has no lines; nor has Grey, whom some modern editors include in the royal party. A director must not only provide blocking for Catesby and Grey (if he is included), but suggest appropriate gestures and movements. (Later, in III.i, Catesby is present for 165 lines before he utters a word.) Similarly, in *All's Well That Ends Well*, V.i, Diana has no lines or stage directions for anything other than her entrance and exit. The original texts give no exit for Edmund in *King Lear*, I.i: does he leave with his father, Gloucester, who is sent to fetch France and Burgundy at line 35, as most modern additions indicate; or does he remain on stage, silently observing the proceedings, until nearly everyone else leaves at line 266? It is a nice question.

3 *Shakespeare Quarterly*, 37 (Spring 1986), 116.

4 Another piece of stage business invented for this production. Dr. Robert Smallwood of the Shakespeare Institute in Stratford-upon-Avon was the first, to my knowledge, to suggest the interpretation of Hippolyta's dream.

5 The Folio text almost certainly represents a revised version of the play, possibly for a revival produced by the King's Men at the Blackfriars Theatre sometime after December 1609, when Middleton's play, *The Witch*, failed. See W. J. Lawrence, *Shakespeare's Workshop* (Oxford: Basil Blackwell, 1928), pp.24-38, and J. M. Nosworthy, *Shakespeare's Occasional Plays* (London: Edward Arnold, 1965), pp. 22 ff. Who made

the revisions, which include the interpolations of two of Middleton's songs from *The Witch*, is not certain, although Nosworthy and others believe Shakespeare could have been and probably was responsible, and not Middleton or some other writer.

6 *The Masks of Macbeth* (Berkeley and Los Angeles: University of California Press, 1978), p. 442.

7 Richard David, *Shakespeare in the Theatre* (Cambridge: Cambridge University Press, 1978), p. 202.

8 Ibid., p. 120.

9 Ibid., p. 88.

10 Philip C. McGuire, *Speechless Dialect: Shakespeare's Open Silences* (Berkeley and Los Angeles: University of California Press, 1985), pp. 39-41.

11 Ibid., pp. 50-55.

12 Ibid., p. 59.

13 Cp. John Russell Brown, *Shakespeare's Plays in Performance* (London: Edward Arnold, 1966; rpt. Harmondsworth: Penguin Books, 1969), p. 56. (Reference is to the reprint.)

14 Franco Zeffirelli's film of the play also used new music, but there the problem was different. Since the film retained the setting of Renaissance Italy, the music had to fit both that setting and the demands of twentieth-century popular music, that is, it also had to satisfy the tastes of the mass audience for whom the film was made.

15 *The Impossible Theater: A Manifesto* (New York: Macmillan, 1964), pp. 280-281.

16 Ibid., p. 284.

17 Ibid., p. 285.

18 Cp. Roger Manvell and John Huntley, *The Technique of Film Music* (London and New York: Focal Press, 1957), p. 61: 'Music, in fact, can become the short cut to emotion'.

19 Roger Manvell, *Shakespeare and the Film* (London: Dent, 1971), pp. 43-44.

20 Grigori Kozintsev, *King Lear: The Space of Tragedy*, tr. Mary Mackintosh (Berkeley and Los Angeles: University of California Press, 1977), p. 247.

Chapter VII

1 *Peter Hall's Diaries*, ed. John Goodwin (London: Hamish Hamilton, 1983), p. 149.

2 In *William Shakespeare: His World, His Work, His Influence*, ed. John Andrews (New York: Scribner's, 1985), III, 818-819.

3 *Free Shakespeare* (London: Heinemann, 1974), p. 11.

4 'Theatrical Shakespearegresses at the Guthrie and Elsewhere: Notes on "Legitimate Production"', *New Literary History*, 17 (1985-86), 511-538, esp. p. 533.

5 *The London Times*, April 21, 1983; cited by Clayton, p. 522. Caird was, in fact, not the first to direct *Twelfth Night* as a dark comedy; a dozen years earlier, Jonathan Miller directed a more extreme version of the play, acted by the Oxford-Cambridge undergraduate players. Peter Hall and John Barton have also directed the play to emphasize its 'autumnal' setting and melancholia: see Trevor Nunn's comments, *On Directing Shakespeare*, ed. Ralph Berry (New York: Barnes & Noble, 1977), p. 60.

6 *Free Shakespeare*, pp. 36-37.

7 According to Gerald M. Berkowitz, 'Shakespeare at the Edinburgh Festival', *Shakespeare Quarterly*, 37 (1986), 228-9)

8 For a discussion of the ambiguities of interpretation in this play, see Norman Rabkin, *Shakespeare and the Problem of Meaning* (Chicago: University of Chicago Press, 1981), pp. 33-62.

9 Cp. Trevor Nunn's discussion of the difficulties in presenting the role in performance, *On Directing Shakespeare*, p. 65.

10 See John Barton, *Playing Shakespeare* (London: Methuen, 1984), pp. 191-192; cited by Clayton, pp. 514-515.

11 *On Directing Shakespeare*, p. 76.

12 *Shakespeare on the Stage* (Boston: Little, Brown, 1973), pp. 199-200.

13 *Free Shakespeare*, p. 53.

14 Ibid., pp. 76-77.

15 See Richard L. Stern, *John Gielgud Directs Richard Burton in 'Hamlet'* (New York: Random House, 1967), p. 329.

16 Constantin Stanislavski, *Building a Character*, tr. Elizabeth Reynolds Hapgood (New York: Theatre Arts Books, 1949), p. 174.

17 Ibid., p. 258.

18 'Stratford Festival Canada', *Shakespeare Quarterly*, 34 (1983), 95-6.

BIBLIOGRAPHY

Abrams, Richard, 'The Doubling of Cordelia and Lear's Fool', *Texas Studies in Language and Literature*, 27 (1985), 354-368.

Andrews, John, ed., *William Shakespeare: His World, His Work, His Influence*, New York: Scribner's, 1985, 3 vols.

Barton, John, *Playing Shakespeare*, London: Methuen, 1984.

Beckerman, Bernard, *Shakespeare at the Globe, 1599-1609*, New York: Macmillan, 1962.

Berry, Ralph, *Changing Styles in Shakespeare*, London: George Allen & Unwin, 1981.

——, ed., *On Directing Shakespeare: Interviews with Contemporary Directors*, New York: Barnes & Noble, 1977.

Blau, Herbert, *The Impossible Theater: A Manifesto*, New York: Macmillan, 1964.

Brockbank, Philip, ed., *Players of Shakespeare*, Cambridge: Cambridge University Press, 1985.

Brooks, Cleanth, *The Well Wrought Urn*, New York: Harcourt, Brace: 1947.

Brown, John Russell, 'S. Franco Zeffirelli's *Romeo and Juliet*', *Shakespeare Survey* 15 (1962). Reprinted in *Shakespeare's Plays in Performance*, London: Edward Arnold, 1966.

——, *Free Shakespeare*, London: Heinemann, 1974.

——, *Shakespeare's Plays in Performance*, London: Edward Arnold, 1966; reprint: Harmondsworth: Penguin Books, 1969.

Carlisle, Carol Jones, *Shakespeare from the Greenroom*, Chapel Hill: University of North Carolina Press, 1969.

Clayton, Thomas, 'Theatrical Shakespearegresses at the Guthrie and Elsewhere: Notes on "Legitimate Production" ', *New Literary History*, 17 (1985-86), 511-538.

Coghill, Nevill, 'Comic Form in *Measure for Measure*', *Shakespeare Survey*, 8 (1955), 14-27.

Cook, Judith, *Shakespeare's Players*, London: Harrap, 1983.

Cox, C. B., and D. J. Palmer, *Shakespeare's Wide and Universal Stage*, Manchester: Manchester University Press, 1984.

David, Richard, *The Janus of the Poets*, New York: Macmillan; Cambridge: Cambridge University Press, 1935.

——, *Shakespeare in the Theatre*, Cambridge: Cambridge University Press, 1978.

Dessen, Alan, *Elizabethan Stage Conventions and Modern Interpreters*, Cambridge: Cambridge University Press, 1984.

Doran, Madeleine, *Shakespeare's Dramatic Language*, Madison: University of Wisconsin Press, 1976.

Fergusson, Francis, *The Idea of a Theater*, Princeton: Princeton University Press, 1949; reprint: Anchor Books, 1953.

Gilder, Rosamund, *John Gielgud's 'Hamlet': A Record of Performance*, Oxford: Oxford University Press, 1937.

Goldman, Michael, *Shakespeare and the Energies of Drama*, Princeton: Princeton University Press, 1972.

Goodwin, John, ed., *Peter Hall's Diaries*, London: Hamish Hamilton, 1983.

Granville-Barker, Harley, *Prefaces to Shakespeare*, Princeton: Princeton University Press, 1946, 2 vols.

Greenwald, Michael, *Directions by Indirections: John Barton of the Royal Shakespeare Company*, Newark: University of Delaware Press, 1985.

Guthrie, Tyrone, *In Various Directions: A View of Theatre*, New York: Macmillan, 1965.

Halio, Jay L., 'Zeffirelli's *Romeo and Juliet:* The Camera versus the Text', *Literature/Film Quarterly*, 5 (Fall 1977), 322-325.

Jorgens, Jack J., *Shakespeare on Film*, Bloomington: Indiana University Press, 1977.

Kirschbaum, Leo, 'Banquo and Edgar: Character or Function?' *Essays in Criticism*, 17 (1957), 1-21.

Kökeritz, Helge, *Shakespeare's Pronunciation*, New Haven: Yale University Press, 1953.

Kozintsev, Grigori, *King Lear: The Space of Tragedy*, tr. Mary Mackintosh, Berkeley and Los Angeles: University of California Press, 1977.

——, *Shakespeare: Time and Conscience*, tr. Joyce Vining, New York: Hill and Wang, 1966.

Lawrence, W. J., *Shakespeare's Workshop*, Oxford: Basil Blackwell, 1928.

Mahood, M. M., *Shakespeare's Wordplay*, London: Methuen, 1957.

Manvell, Roger, *Shakespeare and the Film*, London: Dent, 1971.

Manvell, Roger, and John Huntley, *The Technique of Film Music*, London and New York: Focal Press, 1957.

Maxwell, J. C., 'Shakespeare: The Middle Plays', *A Guide to English Literature: The Age of Shakespeare*, ed. Boris Ford, Balti,more: Penguin Books, 1955.

McGuire, Philip C., *Speechless Dialect: Shakespeare's Open Silences*, Berkeley and Los Angeles: University of California Press, 1985.

Miller, Jonathan, 'Shakespeare and the Modern Director', *William Shakespeare: His World, His Work, His Influence*, ed. John Andrews, New York: Scribner's, 1985, III, 815-822.

Morgan, Joyce Vining, *Stanislavski's Encounter with Shakespeare*, Ann Arbor, MI: UMI Research Press, 1984.

Nosworthy, J. M., *Shakespeare's Occasional Plays: Their Origin and Transmission*, London: Edward Arnold, 1965.

Olivier, Laurence, *On Acting*, New York: Simon and Schuster, 1986.

Price, Joseph G., ed., *The Triple Bond: Plays, Mainly Shakespearean, in Performance*, University Park: Pennsylvania State University Press, 1975.

Rabkin, Norman, *Shakespeare and the Problem of Meaning*, Chicago: University of Chicago Press, 1981.

Ringler, William, 'Shakespeare and His Actors: Some Remarks on *King Lear*', in *Shakespeare's Art from a Comparative Perspective*, ed. W. M. Aycock, Lubbock: Texas Tech Press, 1981, pp. 188-190.

Rosenberg, Marvin, *The Masks of King Lear*, Berkeley and Los Angeles: University of California Press, 1972.

——, *The Masks of Macbeth*, Berkeley and Los Angeles: University of California Press, 1978.

Selbourne, David, *The Making of a Midsummer Night's Dream*, London: Methuen, 1982.

Senelik, Laurence, *Gordon Craig's Moscow 'Hamlet'*, Westport, CT 1982.

Shakespeare, William, *Hamlet* (1676). A Facsimile Published by Cornmarket Press from the Copy in the Birmingham Shakespeare Library, London, 1969.

Sher, Antony, *Year of the King: An Actor's Diary and Sketchbook*, London: Chatto & Windus, 1985; reprinted in paperback by Methuen.

Slater, Ann Pasternak, *Shakespeare the Director*, Sussex: Harvester Press; New Jersey: Barnes & Noble, 1982.

Speaight, Robert, *Shakespeare on the Stage*, Boston: Little, Brown, 1973.

Sprague, Arthur Colby, and J. C. Trewin, *Shakespeare's Plays Today*, Columbia: University of South Carolina Press, 1970.

Spurgeon, Caroline, *Shakespeare's Imagery and What It Tells Us*, Cambridge: Cambridge University Press, 1935.

Stanislavski, Constantin, *An Actor Prepares*, tr. Elizabeth Reynolds Hapgood, New York: Theatre Arts Books, 1936.

——, *Building a Character*, tr. Elizabeth Reynolds Hapgood, New York: Theatre Arts Books, 1949.

Stern, Richard L., *John Gielgud Directs Richard Burton in 'Hamlet'*, New York: Random House, 1967.

Styan, J. L., *Shakespeare in Performance: All's Well That Ends Well*, Manchester: Manchester University Press, 1984.

——, *The Shakespeare Revolution: Criticism and Performance in the Twentieth Century*, Cambridge: Cambridge University Press, 1977.

Sullivan, Patrick J., 'Strumpet Wind – The National Theatre's *Merchant of Venice*', *Educational Theatre Journal*, 26 (March 1974), 31-44.

Warren, Michael, and Gary Taylor, eds., *The Division of the Kingdoms*, London: Oxford University Press, 1983.

Weiner Albert B., ed., *Hamlet: The First Quarto, 1603*, Great Neck, NY: Barron's Educational Series, 1962.

Williamson, Jane, 'The Duke and Isabella on the Modern Stage', *The Triple Bond*, ed. Joseph G. Price, University Park: Pennsylvania State University Press, 1975.

INDEX

Spurgeon, Caroline 91
Stanislavski, Constantin 39-40, 48-9, 80-1, 90, 93
Stauffer, Donald 91
Stern, Richard L. 93
Stevenson, Juliet 73
Stewart, Patrick 12, 33, 35-6, 89
Styan, J. L. 33, 89
Suchet, David 12, 33-6, 53
Sullivan, Patrick J. 86

Tamburlaine 74
Taming of the Shrew, The 63
Taylor, Gary 86
Tempest, The 33-4, 42-3, 67-8, 76, 81
Throne of Blood 18
Time of Your Life,The 73
Tree, Herbert Beerbohm 20
Trewin, J. C. 87
Troilus and Cressida 20-1, 26, 67, 72
Twelfth Night 75-6, 92
Two Gentlemen of Verona, The 13

Ultz 24

Vining, Joyce 89; as Joyce Vining Morgan 96

Waller, David 67
Walton, William 71
Warren, Michael 86
Warren, Roger 65, 74
Waterston, Sam 27
Weiner, Albert B. 86
Welles, Orson 61
Wells, Stanley 86, 87
Wickham, Chrissy 70
Widdoes, Kathleen 14, 26, 58
Williams, Clifford 33
Williamson, Jane 46, 90
Williamson, Nicoll 42, 66
Wilson, Stuart 67
Wilton, Penelope 46
Winter's Tale, The 34-5, 70-1
Witch, The 21, 91

Young, Charles 21
Young, Vic 29
Your Own Thing 29

Zeffirelli, Franco 16, 92